D0466951

WASHINGTON DECEASED

Also by Michael Bowen:

Can't Miss
Badger Game

WASHINGTON DECEASED

A Mystery

M
C2

MICHAEL BOWEN

(ST. MARTIN'S PRESS)1990
New York

To R. L. in Bethesda,
with many thanks

WASHINGTON DECEASED. Copyright © 1990 by Michael Bowen. All
rights reserved. Printed in the United States of America. No part of
this book may be used or reproduced in any manner whatsoever without
written permission except in the case of brief quotations embodied in
critical articles or reviews. For information, address St. Martin's Press,
175 Fifth Avenue, New York, N.Y. 10010

Design by Amelia R. Mayone

Library of Congress Cataloging-in-Publication Data

Bowen, Michael.
        Washington deceased / by Michael Bowen.
                p.   cm.
        ISBN 0-312-05179-4
        I. Title.
    PS3552.0864W3   1990
    813'.54—dc20   90-37232
                                                                 CIP

First Edition

10 9 8 7 6 5 4 3 2 1

"Washington is full of famous men and the women they married when they were young."

—Fanny Holmes

".... *tous les combats politiques sont douteux. Ce n'est jamais la lutte entre le bien et le mal, c'est le préférable contre le détestable.*"

(".... all political battle is dubious. It is never a struggle between good and evil, but between the preferable and the detestable.")

—Raymond Aron, *Le Spectateur Engagé*, pp. 289–90 (Julliard, Paris 1981)

Floor Plan, Honor Cottage B-4 (First Floor)

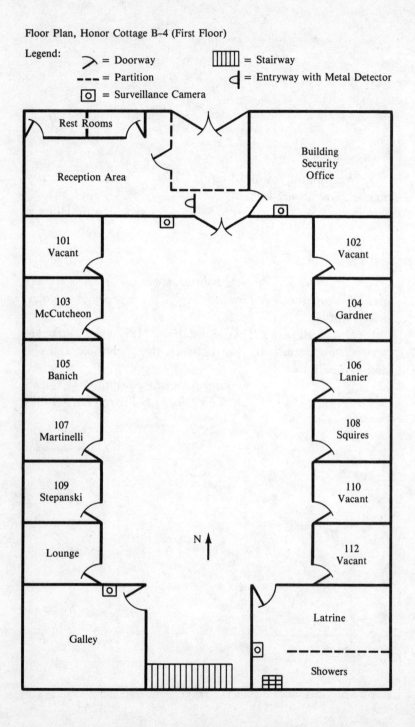

Floor Plan, Honor Cottage B-4 (Basement)

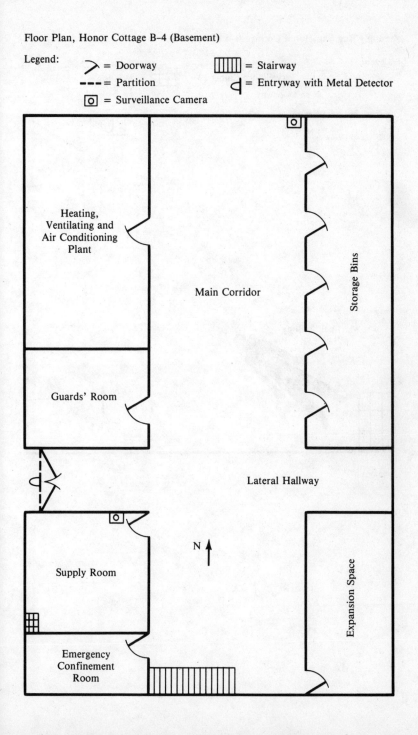

Supply Room in Honor Cottage B-4 (Basement)

Legend:

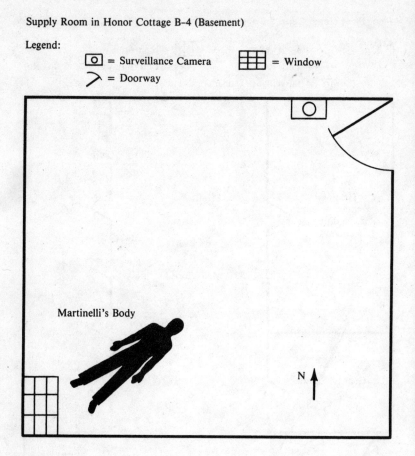

CHAPTER 1

The human body isn't designed to survive collision with eight grams of lead moving twenty-five hundred feet per second, and Sweet Tony Martinelli's body didn't. His extinction had both positive and negative implications for former United States Senator Desmond Gardner. On the plus side, it perceptibly improved the immediate quality of Gardner's life. On the other hand, Gardner thought it might interfere with his parole application.

Gardner had already gotten Richard Michaelson involved by the time Sweet Tony bought it, so the story has to start at a time when he was still alive.

About ten minutes before noon on the last full day of Martinelli's life, Wendy Gardner hurried down Connecticut toward Massachusetts Avenue where she would turn left and, she hoped, quickly find the Brookings Institution. Two or three undisciplined clusters of blond hair strayed over her forehead.

In her left arm she cradled a sack holding a thin, hardcover book she had just bought. Its title was *Bright Lines and Slippery Slopes: Nine Fallacies in Current Foreign Policy Discourse*. Richard Michaelson had written it. A true child of Washington, Wendy had stopped to buy the improbably named

1

volume, even though she was running late and didn't have the slightest intention of ever reading it. She thought that she might ingratiate herself with Michaelson by having a copy of it with her when she met him.

Wendy Gardner was at this time a sophomore at the principal public university of the midwestern state that her father had served for eleven years in the United States Senate. She was five-and-a-half feet tall and would just have nudged into the featherweight class had she boxed—an activity for which she had the disposition but not the aptitude.

She had the virtues of her deficiencies. She was tolerant and open-minded, to the point of regarding "everything's relative" as a dogmatic, all-purpose moral judgment. Viewing recreational sex as immature and promiscuity as irresponsible, she thought that sexual intimacy should be confined to relationships involving love and commitment. She had been in love five times. Liberated from the stranglehold of juvenile idealism, she saw herself as an unflinching, hard-bitten realist, gazing cold-eyed and without comfort of illusion on the world as it was.

This was like viewing Sylvester Stallone as a commando: It was possible only until she met the real thing.

Which she was about to do.

CHAPTER 2

Arriving too late to be introduced to Michaelson before the start of the Brookings colloquy where she was supposed to meet him, Wendy found herself sitting against the wall of a windowless conference room in a standard-issue Washington office suite, watching the confabulation itself proceed. Michaelson sat at the head of a long, blunted-oval table that dominated the room. He had snow-white hair and tight, chiseled features, as if in his long association with Washington his face had come to resemble the city's less derivative statuary. His fair skin, untanned and unburned, set off eyes so dark brown they seemed to Wendy to be black. Except for the pinkie on his left hand, half of which was missing, his fingers were long and elegant. Wendy correctly surmised from the fingers that Michaelson was tall—about six-two, in fact—and that when he stood his rather spare frame would make him seem even taller.

Fooled by the hair, Wendy guessed that Michaelson was near sixty-five. He had actually just turned fifty-seven. Had she seen him on the street, in his brown-tone tweed suit, white shirt and brown-and-mustard bow tie, she would have guessed that he was a professor at George Washington University or a lobbyist for the American Association of Retired Persons.

Around the rest of the table sat six men and three women.

They seemed to Wendy incredibly young—early to middle twenties, all of them—and Wendy thought that they looked like wonks. When Michaelson spoke they took notes with the kind of bizarre intensity that Wendy associated with the tools in Survey of English Literature who really cared about whether John Donne was a better poet than Richard Lovelace.

She wouldn't have guessed that these people were all on campaign staffs. And she would never have imagined that, within thirty months or so, one or more of them would probably be helping a President elect of the United States pick a covey of senior advisors.

As she got settled, one of the wonks was finishing a question.

"—and so do you feel you have exposed the moral bankruptcy of the policy of constructive engagement toward South Africa?"

"No. What I have tried to expose is the logical incoherence of the stated rationale for that policy," Michaelson said. His voice was low and resonant, his cadence unhurried, his tone dry and detached.

"The premise of your argument being, however, that the continued existence of apartheid is unacceptable."

"The premise of my argument is that the continued existence of apartheid is unlikely. 'Unacceptable' is a term that I wouldn't use in that context."

"Why not?"

"Because when you are doing foreign policy I don't think that you should say something is unacceptable unless you mean it."

"In the case of South Africa, some of us do mean it."

"I doubt that very much."

"Believe it," the wonk persisted. "Some of us are prepared to recommend complete diplomatic isolation and full-scale trade sanctions."

"Fair enough," Michaelson nodded. "But if you take those

steps and they don't put an end to apartheid and white minority rule in South Africa, what do you do then?"

"You've done all you can do."

"I think not," Michaelson replied. "There are certainly other things you *could* do: military aid to insurgents; U.S. air and naval blockade; invasion of South Africa by U.S. military forces; and so forth. The question is, are you really willing to do them?"

"Not all of them, certainly."

"Nor am I. I take it then we can agree that apartheid and white minority rule are lamentable and reprehensible but not unacceptable since, under certain circumstances, you would accept them."

"But in that sense there's nothing that's unacceptable, is there?" someone else asked.

"Nothing except impairment of the sovereignty, political independence or territorial integrity of the United States. But that's a rather critical exception, isn't it?"

It seemed to Wendy that Michaelson was being rather rude to his young interlocutors. She wondered why they all seemed not just respectful but actually rather taken with him. What Wendy saw as rudeness, however, was Michaelson's refusal to condescend to the people he was talking to. He knew exactly what they wanted to hear and he understood perfectly well how to say it and make it ring with conviction. Instead of doing that, he was telling them what he really thought.

Vaguely uncomfortable with what she was hearing, Wendy stopped paying attention to the conversation and sought distraction in Michaelson's book.

She turned first to the back flap of the dust jacket, where she saw a flattering halftone of Michaelson and a one-paragraph biography that emphasized the positions he had held before retiring after thirty-five years in the Foreign Service: consul, desk officer, commercial attaché, political counsellor, desk officer again but this time for a country she had heard of, deputy chief of mission and area director. None of them sounded like very exciting jobs. She didn't notice that there weren't quite enough of them to add up to thirty-five years of active duty in the Foreign Service.

She shrugged and opened at random to the text. "The oft-heard prescription that, 'The United States should prefer negotiation to military force,' " she read, "exemplifies the fallacy of the false alternative. The use of force isn't an alternative to negotiation; it is a form of negotiation."

Wendy blinked and shook her head. She closed the book and decided to pay more attention to the discussion.

"You described the premise of your position as being that the continued existence of apartheid is unlikely," a wonk not heard from up to now was saying. "I take it then you believe that, eventually, majority rule in South Africa is inevitable."

"If by majority rule you mean rule by a minority that is the same color as the majority of people in the country, then I think it is quite likely indeed."

"In other words, since blacks are going to be running things in South Africa in the foreseeable future, the time to get on the winning side is now."

"Yes. As Damon Runyon put it, the race may not be always to the swift, nor the battle to the strong—but that's the way to bet."

"Would you allow any role to *moral* value judgments in making foreign policy?"

"To one, at least."

"Namely?"

"That in the struggle between freedom and tyranny, freedom should win."

"That is, freedom should win globally—even at the cost of important values in particular places."

"That is correct."

"So that national interest excuses a multitude of sins."

"Yes. But one sin national interest never excuses is believing your own propaganda."

———

"That's really what you're saying is wrong with constructive engagement, isn't it?" Wonk 1 asked. "That it's based on believing our own propaganda."

"Exactly," Michaelson said, his voice suddenly quieter. "The present policy is sentimental, based on the fond but groundless hope that a choice implicating the knowing acceptance of evil will never have to be made. That isn't the way the world is. At the level of superpower rivalry, foreign policy is carried out in a pure, Hobbesian state of nature: a pitiless struggle of all against all, conducted without law, without faith, and without joy."

Wendy Gardner sat unnoticed in an eerie stillness as the colloquy continued. She had walked into the room thinking that Richard Michaelson was probably a pedantic, curmudgeonly old fart. She no longer thought that. She now thought he was a cold, Machiavellian monster. Her gut churned at the thought of asking him for anything.

Notwithstanding which, as the conference wound down, she braced herself to do exactly that.

"Senator Gardner's daughter?" Michaelson asked a bit later when she had finally been able to make her way to him.

"Yes."

"This is a delightful surprise, Ms. Gardner. I've known Desmond Gardner for many years. There are a couple of stories about us that I hear are still being told in the diplomatic and political worlds."

Wendy's spirits sank a bit. Outside his state, where his name still held some magic, people had tended since Gardner's conviction and imprisonment to downplay or altogether forget their past associations with him. She concluded that Michaelson must have forgotten that her father was a convicted felon, and that any inclination Michaelson had to help would cool as soon as she brought that complicating detail up.

"Good," Wendy said, forging ahead. "You see—"

7

"He's at Fritchieburg now, isn't he?"

"Yes," Wendy stammered, surprised at this colloquial reference to the Federal Minimum Security Correctional Facility outside Fritchieburg, Maryland, where her father was an inmate.

"Excuse me for interrupting. You were about to say something."

Wendy took a deep breath and prepared to launch into the rapid but detailed explanation of her father's plight that she had gotten ready to try to keep Michaelson from telling her no before she could get the salient facts out.

"He sent me to ask for your help, so I'm cutting the last week of classes before spring break to come out here. You see, he's afraid that he's getting squeezed for some information that he doesn't have and that his parole could be jeopardized by something that's going on that he doesn't understand."

"I'll be glad to—"

"He's even afraid that he may be in physical danger," Wendy continued. "I could tell over the phone that he was upset, and there seem to be a lot of people in Washington who can't remember who he was anymore. He told me to come to you and see, ah—"

"I said yes," Michaelson interjected gently as Wendy groped for her next word.

She managed to choke off the flow of sounds and look up. "Excuse me?"

"The answer is yes. I'll help Senator Gardner in any way that I can. As I said, he and I go back a long way." Michaelson glanced at his watch. "Let's find a sandwich and talk this over in the sunshine."

CHAPTER 3

"Looks like something's going on up there," Wendy said, nodding toward DuPont Circle a hundred yards away. She and Michaelson were walking along Massachusetts Avenue toward the circle. In paper bags they carried delicatessen sandwiches and half pint cartons of milk.

"They have demonstrations there all the time," Michaelson remarked. "Often some fellows with orange turbans. The Indian Embassy is fairly close, and the chaps with the turbans seem to be cranky about something or other that the Indian government has done."

"This looks like it must be a different group."

"I believe you're right. I don't see any turbans."

The demonstration was taking place primarily on the other side of the non-functional fountain in the middle, and so it was only when Wendy and Michaelson had crossed the street and actually entered DuPont Circle that they were able to determine the nature of the demonstrators' cause.

"Animal rights," Wendy said.

Michaelson could read picket signs agitated by two of the demonstrators. One said, "Carnivores Are Cannibals." The other said, "Meat Is for Meatheads." A young woman hustled around the circle and thrust a handbill toward them.

"Thank you *very* much," Michaelson said, accepting it enthusiastically.

Picking their way past three sets of chess players and a greasy-tressed youth playing a guitar, Wendy and Michaelson found their way to a concrete bench on the perimeter of the circle. Michaelson laid the handbill face down on the bench and invited Wendy to sit on it. As soon as she did, he straddled the bench, about a yard away from her.

"Tell me more about what I can do for your father," he said as he opened his sack.

"Like I said, he's afraid he's getting squeezed for information he doesn't have."

"Why is he afraid of that?"

"The U.S. Attorney from back home sent someone out to see him about a month ago. The guy who came out implied that dad must know something about a big corruption thing that supposedly happened a couple of years ago or so. Dad's served almost seventeen months of his sentence. He's up for parole in two months. The guy who came out said that if dad didn't cooperate in this further investigation, the U.S. Attorney would oppose his parole application."

"I see. What's the nature of the information he's supposed to have?"

"They wouldn't tell him. The guy just said something like, 'Think about sugar and see if your memory comes back.' "

"Sounds like a script from a bad movie."

"There's something more," Wendy said.

"What's that?"

"He thinks he may be in danger."

"You mentioned that. Why does he think so?"

"He said he couldn't tell me." Wendy looked away from Michaelson. Her cheeks flushed. "He asked me to see if I could get you to come out and talk to him. Not on the phone, he said. Face to face."

Michaelson nodded.

"Could we do it this afternoon?" he asked.

10

Wendy looked back at him, startled. She had thought that, if everything went perfectly, *maybe* she could get Michaelson out to see her father in a week.

"No visiting in the afternoon," she said. "Tomorrow morning would be the earliest."

"Tomorrow morning, then. Where are you staying?"

"Hartnett Hall."

"I know it. I'll pick you up out front at 7:15. That should get us there comfortably by 9:00."

"Great. I mean, thank you."

"You're welcome. Before we go out there, there's something you could do yet today. Go to the Library of Congress and see if you can put together a list of the members of Congress who were on the Subcommittees on Western Hemisphere Trade of the International Commerce Committees in the House and Senate for the period from two to five years ago. Also everyone on the staffs of each member."

"Okay," Wendy said. "But what makes you think those names will be useful? You don't even know what the problem is yet."

"True enough," Michaelson agreed. "But we know that it involves sugar, and we know it involves Congress. Those subcommittees seem like a good place to start."

Wendy glanced over at the demonstration as she began to attack her sandwich. A short man with wiry black hair was using a bullhorn to address the sign-waving throng. He had already harangued them and led them in antiphonal chants. Now he gestured over to a U-Haul trailer parked illegally at the edge of the circle and eyed skeptically by a brace of D.C. motorcycle officers. Over the bullhorn he promised the sign wavers that soon—*soon*—they would all expose graphically the agony to which innocent animals were subjected in order to satisfy the human species' unhealthy craving for meat.

"I wonder what the problem is," Wendy said, referring to the demonstration. "It looks like they've run out of steam and are improvising."

"I've been wondering the same thing," Michaelson commented. "They probably have something visual planned for the climax, but they can't do it until the TV cameras arrive."

The man with the bullhorn began slowly to circle the fountain, looking for something new to rev up the demonstrators' flagging enthusiasm.

Wendy shrugged and turned back to face Michaelson.

"You were in the Foreign Service for quite a while," she said, trying to make conversation.

"Thirty-five years," he confirmed.

"Why did you leave?"

"Good question." Michaelson squinted toward Georgetown. He was used to making quick tactical decisions, and he decided now on tactical grounds to tell Wendy Gardner the truth. He reasoned that if Desmond Gardner's problem was half as serious as it sounded, Wendy would be hearing the truth about Michaelson from someone before long. "It was sort of a gamble."

"What do you mean by that?"

"When I finished my tour as Area Director for Near East and South Asian Affairs, I sat back and looked at what I had still available to me in the Service. It boiled down to a rather vague hope that if things broke just the right way I might be able to exchange the handful of political chits I had for a promotion one or two rungs up from the regular civil service."

"You have political chits?"

"A few."

"How did you get those?"

"The usual ways. A couple of once and future presidential candidates sounded marginally less moronic on several foreign policy questions during the last campaign than they would have without my discreet contributions. I saw to it that one or two senators on the Intelligence Oversight Committee knew they were being lied to twelve hours before the *Washington Post* did."

"And you thought you might be able to cash in on that?"

"I had at least a prospect of doing so. If I'd stayed with the Service I could not unreasonably have hoped for an ambassadorship to one of the countries traditionally reserved for professionals rather than political appointees, or perhaps a senior administrative post—AID Director, that kind of thing. If I were very, very lucky, I could get Deputy Under Secretary of State, or even Under Secretary. Failing any of those, however, I'd just be a Senior Counselor until retirement."

"That idea didn't appeal to you?"

He shrugged noncommittally. "I decided to go for the gold ring, so to speak."

"By retiring?"

"By retiring. Getting a sinecure at Brookings. Writing a little book for the cognoscenti. Giving talks to insiders. Having chats over lunch with syndicated columnists. Writing an op ed piece every now and then. Consulting with promising campaigns. Engaging generally in shameless self-promotion."

"The idea being what?"

"To see if, when administrations change, I could obtain one of the top three foreign policy-making positions available to an unelected American citizen: National Security Adviser, Secretary of Defense or Director of the Central Intelligence Agency."

Wendy blinked. "Not Secretary of State?"

"It's no use being Secretary of State unless you've made your mark already in one of the three posts I just named. Absent that, the United States Secretary of State has less functional authority than a bird colonel in the White House basement."

"Is your plan working?"

Michaelson smiled.

"Time will tell," he said.

"There's something I think I should tell you," Wendy said. "You've been very kind to agree to help and everything, but—" She hesitated.

13

"If you think you should tell me something, then by all means do."

Wendy sat back and forced herself to make eye contact with him.

"I thought that what you were saying back at Brookings about apartheid was appalling."

"I agree. The truth often is."

Before they could pursue this topic, the young man with the bullhorn interrupted them. He had noticed defections from the rear ranks of his followers, and there still wasn't a minicam in sight. He was casting about desperately for something to hold the demonstration together for a few more minutes, and when he saw what Wendy and Michaelson were eating he decided he'd found it.

"Do you know how much suffering went into that veal you're eating?" he demanded of Wendy.

"It's chicken," she said mildly.

"It's still meat," the man asserted.

"I beg your pardon," Michaelson interjected, "but it's not, you know."

"What?" the man squeaked, turning toward Michaelson.

"Meat is the flesh of a mammal," Michaelson explained. "Like this." He flourished what remained of his roast beef sandwich. "Chickens aren't mammals. Therefore, chicken isn't meat. You were mistaken."

"Then what about what you're eating? Do you realize that to produce that sandwich a helpless calf had to suffer unspeakably. . . ."

"Oh, no doubt," Michaelson shrugged. "But of course it is only my enjoyment of this sandwich that gives meaning to that creature's suffering. If I weren't eating this sandwich, the steer whose fate you bemoan would have lived, suffered and died for nothing."

To this outrageous proposition the wiry-haired man could conceive only one rebuttal. This was to put his bullhorn as close to Michaelson's ear as he could manage and scream "Cannibal!" at him.

He raised the bullhorn for this purpose, but that was as far as he got. Irritated at the intrusion and furious at the impending incivility, Wendy bobbed up and stuffed the remains of her chicken sandwich into the bullhorn's muzzle. She did this with considerable vigor, so that she not only reduced the roar from the instrument to a pathetic, tinny bleat, but also forced the mouthpiece brusquely against the aggressor's lips and teeth, cutting the former and chipping the latter.

It wasn't clear what turn the confrontation would have taken had a policeman not intervened by tapping the man with the bullhorn on the shoulder.

"Excuse me," the policeman said. "Are you the one in charge of that trailer over there?" He pointed toward the U-Haul.

"Yes," the man said, rather happy to shift his defiance from the blazing-eyed young woman to the armed cop.

"I'm going to have to give you a citation."

"What for?" the man sneered. He began to hope that this disaster might be salvaged yet. He raised his voice. "What pretext have you invented for interfering with our peaceful assembly? Disturbing the peace? Inciting to riot?"

The demonstrators hooted appreciatively at these absurd possibilities.

"No," the policeman explained as he began to fill out the ticket. "Cruelty to animals."

"What?"

The man looked over his shoulder in time to see two other policemen snap the lock on the trailer and rescue from its steamy inside a calf in a simulated holding pen that the man had been saving to impress the media. Unfortunately, the media chose only now to appear, and began videotaping the heroic efforts of the police officers to save the wobbly-legged calf from the nearly fatal effects of dehydration and overheating it had suffered at the hands of the animal rights activists.

"Do you mind if I ask you something?" Wendy said when she and Michaelson had finished viewing the spectacle.

"Go ahead."

"What happened to the little finger on your left hand?"

"I lost most of it in an accident," Michaelson said dismissively. "What you did with the sandwich just now was marvelous, by the way."

Wendy blushed and shrugged.

"Is that what you meant when you said the use of force is a form of negotiation?" she asked.

"Yes," Michaelson said reflectively. "As a matter of fact it is."

Michaelson's interest in becoming CIA Director would have surprised those of his former colleagues who had known him only by reputation. The Foreign Service looks on the Central Intelligence Agency in much the same way that an old money, East Coast family might look on a ne'er-do-well nephew who had gone to Hollywood and made a fortune producing pornographic films: that is, with a mixture of embarrassment, contempt—and envy.

Henry L. Stimson captured the Foreign Service attitude perfectly when he explained that he had closed the State Department's code-breaking office because gentlemen didn't read each other's mail. Even today, most old school FSO's still try to ignore the colleagues with titles like Water Hygiene Expert or Attaché for Science and Technology Affairs who pass themselves off as embassy staff but who everybody knows are spooks. The FSOs disapprove of supposed subordinates whom the locals believe (often correctly) to have more real power than the U.S. ambassador, and who have their own private communications link—the back channel—for sending Washington messages that the ambassador not only hasn't cleared but doesn't even know about.

Michaelson never shared this attitude. His view was that gentlemen neither read each other's mail nor launched sneak attacks on each other's naval bases, but that this was no excuse for confusing nation states with gentlemen. He thought that espionage was important, he observed that the CIA was good at it, and he was therefore glad that the spooks were there.

The only problem, as he saw it, lay in two nagging CIA deficiencies: an ignorance of local geography—the CIA thought that the United States Department of State was located in Langley, Virginia; and a problem with arithmetic—the CIA thought that the United States had only one branch of government.

The remedy, Michaelson thought, was quite clear. Since the CIA was good at spying on other countries but not good at telling the State Department and Congress everything it found out, the efficient thing for the State Department to do was to spy on the CIA.

This Michaelson had proceeded to do at every duty post where he had enjoyed the requisite authority. He not infrequently tapped the spooks' phone lines, patched into their back channel transmissions, suborned their local operatives, or even stole their typewriter and cable-printer ribbons from the burn bag and held them up to mirrors to read them. More often, he did the less exotic, more tedious things that produce most real intelligence: observing whom the spooks lunched with, analyzing their purchase orders, tracking curious patterns in their personnel assignments and so forth. He'd stopped short at breaking into their embassy precincts and burgling their desks and file cabinets—he wouldn't have known how and, anyway, he never had to.

He was good enough at this that he ultimately spent seven years of his career in charge of the Interagency Liaison and

Assessment Bureau, an office he had created for the purpose of generalizing his approach.

Michaelson made it a point to share the information he obtained. He shared it with his superiors, of course, but also with those of the people's elected representatives who weren't on the payrolls of foreign powers, knew how to keep their mouths shut when reporters were around, and had a decent shot at being president some day. The last criterion suggested to some that Michaelson wasn't wholly motivated in his disclosures by an idealistic commitment to democratic governance. He wasn't—but then, nothing in Washington is ever entirely unambiguous.

CHAPTER 4

As these events were taking place, the afternoon routine in Honor Cottage B-4 of the United States Minimum Security Correctional Facility near Fritchieburg, Maryland, was just getting underway.

Correctional Officer/Grade 2 Wesson Smith was preparing to leave the Building Security Office and take a walk through the Honor Cottage. (Honor Cottage B-4 didn't look anything like a cottage. It had a ground floor and a basement and was about the size and shape of a quonset hut—which, come to think of it, doesn't look anything like a hut.) He turned to the television monitor on his desk and flipped at random through the six closed-circuit video cameras in the building. Finding nothing worthy of note, he stepped in front of the full-length mirror bolted to the rear wall and looked himself over.

He saw razor-sharp creases on his light-brown-with-loden-green-trim uniform shirt and slacks, a gleaming brass buckle on his green web belt and shoes polished to a dazzling shine. Retired after twenty years in the Army, he was now seven years into his second career, with the Federal Bureau of Prisons. Satisfied, he opened the door and stepped out of his office.

This was at the front of the building, on the ground floor. At the back of the building, in the basement, inmate Larry Stepanski had just used a plastic card key to unlock the Supply

19

Room. He led his fellow B-4 inmates inside to give them the things they'd need to do the work assigned to them that afternoon.

"Let's see," Stepanski said in a blast furnace voice as he consulted a clipboard, "whadda you got today, Counsellor Squires?"

"The galley," replied Norman Squires, a sandy-haired, round-shouldered man.

"Galley, right," Stepanski said. "That's what normal people call the kitchen, isn't it?"

Squires reddened while Stepanski offered a good-natured, no offense, Counselor kind of laugh and handed Squires a sponge, a pad of steel wool and a small can of Ajax. Squires took them and left.

"Martinelli, pride of Miami," Stepanski said then with another glance at the clipboard. "I got you down for windows, ground floor lounge."

"Fuck you," Martinelli said.

"Get in line, brother," Stepanski grinned. He kicked in Martinelli's direction a bucket holding a plastic bottle of Windex and a wad of paper towels. "See if you can get 'em dirty this time."

"Up yours," Martinelli said.

"Just think where you'd be without your charm, Martinelli," Stepanski replied, but Martinelli was already out the door.

"I'm down for the baseboards," Leo Banich said.

"Baseboards it is," Stepanski confirmed. He gave Banich a bucket and a white rag. "You don't need any cleanser for that. Just water and elbow grease."

Banich nodded and started to walk out.

"Uh, Banich," Stepanski said gently to him.

"Yeah?" Banich turned back in Stepanski's direction.

"That's a metal bucket, right?"

"Geez, I know it's a metal bucket for chrissake."

"Right. So since it's a metal bucket you're going to empty it out in the john, not outside, okay?"

"Yeah," Banich sighed.

" 'Cause if you try to take that metal bucket through an outside door, the metal detector's gonna go off like a four-alarm fire and probably give CO-2 Smith even more indigestion than he usually has by setting off that godawful buzzer in his office, right?"

"Right," Banich conceded listlessly. And walked out.

"Okay, Senator," Stepanski said then, "whadda you have?"

"Toilet," Desmond Gardner said cheerfully.

"Right you are, Senator. Better watch it, though. CO-2 Smith says we should call it the latrine."

"CO-2 Smith can call it what he likes," Gardner said, saluting toward the camera mounted near the ceiling in the corner of the room where the door was. "I call it the toilet."

Stepanski and Gardner laughed at this modestly spirited defiance as Stepanski gave Gardner a pair of soiled, white-and-blue work gloves and a collection of appropriate implements.

Correctional Officer/Grade 2 Smith didn't like to be called CO-2 Smith. The correct form of address for someone of his rank was Officer. The approved abbreviation for the rank was CO/2nd, *not* CO-2. Naturally, all of the inmates called him CO-2 Smith.

Smith wasn't sure whether this spurious title, with its gaseous allusion, referred to his penchant for platitudinous rhetoric or to his tendency to flatulence. Whichever it was, he didn't appreciate it.

Gardner left and headed for the back stairs, which would take him up one flight to the shower room and toilets near the back of the main floor. He didn't wait to see Terry Lanier and Tommy McCutcheon receive the wherewithal for their assignments.

_____

21

On the floor above Stepanski, Correctional Officer/Grade 2 Smith completed his tour and found nothing amiss.

Stepanski, having finished the assignments for everyone else, poured a mixture of potassium phosphate and calcium into a small plastic drum, sealed it, and attached a plastic hose and spritzer to a valve in the lid. He left the Supply Room, checking after he was out to make sure that the door was locked. He hung his clipboard on a hook near the door. He turned left down a short hallway that intersected the basement's central corridor just before the Supply Room. He went out a side door at the end of that hallway, mounted a flight of iron, outside stairs, and looked for brown patches on the modest lawn around the building to fertilize. He always saved the outside jobs for himself.

Two minutes later, Correctional Officer/Grade 2 Smith started down the back stairs to the basement. He thought he heard a voice. He stopped and listened. He couldn't make out the words, but he was sure he could hear a male voice, coming from the basement.

He went down the stairs as quietly as he could. Someone deaf as a stone probably wouldn't have heard him. He reached the well lit basement and stepped into the central corridor. He couldn't see anyone.

He walked down to the intersecting hallway and looked in both directions. He still couldn't see anyone.

He backtracked to the door of the Supply Room. He listened. He couldn't hear anything. He tried the door. It was locked. Smith was sure he had the only key except for the one that he let Stepanski keep because Stepanski could run the work detail smoothly without hassling Smith. And he knew Stepanski was outside because otherwise the clipboard wouldn't be hanging on the hook by the door.

He took the clipboard off the hook where Stepanski had hung it and briefly examined the duty roster clipped there. He listened some more. He still didn't hear anything. He shrugged and began walking again down the basement corridor toward the front of the building, methodically completing his rounds.

One thing you had to say for Correctional Officer/Grade 2 Smith: He was dumber than a box of rocks.

Desmond Gardner scrubbed ferociously at a mixture of scaley-white and brownish crust on the inside of a toilet bowl. When he had cleared it away, he poured Sani-Flush in the bowl's water until it turned blue. Then he squirted a thin, pink stream of Lysol under the rim of the bowl and quickly swabbed the liquid evenly around the porcelain.

Desmond Gardner enjoyed cleaning toilets. Stepanski knew this and gave the task to him for that reason. When you cleaned toilets, you worked for an hour or so and when you were through you stepped back and saw the tangible results of your efforts. After six years in both state legislative bodies and the United States House of Representatives, eleven years in the United States Senate, two marriages, two divorces and one felony conviction, Desmond Gardner found it gratifying to see in blue water and sparkling porcelain evidence that an hour of his labor had produced unambiguously positive results.

Back upstairs, Correctional Officer/Grade 2 Smith stepped into the Building Security Office. He was frowning at a report from Stepanski stuck on the clipboard behind the duty roster. The report disclosed the disappearance from the Supply Room of a spool of one hundred yards of two hundred-pound test Stren monofilament fishing line. This disappearance vexed Smith, who would now have to beg, borrow or requisition something else to do the work of binding twine and baling wire and—most critical with summer coming—a replacement cutting surface for B-4's weed eater.

———

23

Smith closed the door of the office and automatically checked himself in the mirror. The image wasn't quite as perfect as it had been when he'd checked it fifteen minutes earlier. A smear fogging part of the mirror marred the otherwise stirring reflection.

"Shit," he muttered. "What the hell?"

Smith rubbed ineffectually at the smear with his right sleeve. He repeated the expletive. He looked through the open window a foot away but didn't see Stepanski. He stepped over to his desk and flipped on a microphone that would send his voice over loudspeakers located around the building and on both of the long outside walls.

"Attention," he barked. "Inmate Stepanski, report to Building Security immediately. That is all."

Banich scoured baseboards.

Lanier opened the door of the Supply Room from the inside, glanced cautiously in both directions down the basement corridor, then stepped outside and closed the door behind him. He made sure it was locked. Then he hurried toward the back stairs.

When he had finished cleaning the eight toilets, Gardner carried his paraphernalia around a tiled partition into the shower room. He scrubbed the tiles with nothing but soap and water, putting his back into it and trying to bring a sparkle to them. Then he used a toothbrush to scour the grouting in between the tiles, brushing grime away from the gray-white cement.

He heard the door to the latrine open and close. He stopped what he was doing and listened to steps move across the floor on the other side of the wall. He waited philosophically for the sound of urination, which would symbolize the transience of the work he had just finished. He was surprised when he heard only the very different sound of tap water running in a washbasin.

The latrine door opened and closed again. Gardner couldn't be sure, but he thought he heard a startled gasp from the first man who had come in. The first voice he heard came from the second man. It was Martinelli's.

"Don't worry, Squires, it's just me, not that dumbshit Smith. I won't take away your nose candy."

"Watch what you accuse me of."

This can't be trouble, Gardner thought. If he had anything obnoxious in mind, Martinelli would at least have glanced around the partition to see if anybody else was in here.

"You hurt my feelings, Squires. You stood me up last night."

So much for that theory, Gardner noted mentally. Familiarity breeds contempt. Martinelli's gotten familiar enough with the rest of us not to bother with even elementary precautions anymore.

"We didn't have a date," Squires told Martinelli.

"We have a date when I say we have a date, Squires." Martinelli's voice was low and jovial, but redolent with menace all the same.

"I don't do it with boys."

"You don't understand, Squires. I'm not selling, I'm telling. When I knock on that door tonight, you'd better open up."

"Now listen, you cheap hood—"

"Look who's gettin' tough," Martinelli laughed. "Cheapass shyster, toughest thing you've ever done is crack an egg. You know what your problem is, Squires? You need to get creased up a little bit, that's what your problem is."

Gardner heard the sound of feet moving swiftly across a tile floor and he didn't hesitate. He picked up his bucket and supplies and scurried noisily around the corner.

"Afternoon, gentlemen," he called out.

Martinelli, who held a generous piece of Squires's shirt, glared over his shoulder.

"Take a hike, Gardner."

"I'm not through in here." Gardner put the bucket down.

"I say you are through in here. Take a hike."

"Not 'till I'm finished."

Martinelli let go of Squires and turned around to look at Gardner. Martinelli was hirsute, five-ten and looked like he weighed a solid one hundred-eighty pounds. Gardner was pushing fifty but like many successful politicians he had a surprisingly imposing body. He topped six feet and his build was big but without much fat.

Martinelli turned back to Squires.

"Don't forget what I said," he instructed the cringing former lawyer. He walked out of the latrine.

"What's this I'm looking at, Stepanski?" Correctional Officer/Grade 2 Smith asked.

"I don't know."

"It's your report about the missing fishing line."

"Oh."

"What would anyone want with fishing line?"

"I don't know."

"We're all in this together."

"Yessir."

"One guy can screw it up for everybody."

"Yessir."

"Pass the word."

"Yessir."

"I don't want any more theft."

"Nosir."

"A word to the wise."

"Yessir."

"I want the Lounge and the first floor policed up better tomorrow, and I mean not just swept but dusted."

"Yessir."

"There's too much dust and dirt floating around here."

"Yessir."

"Look at what's happened to my mirror."

Stepanski glanced at the massive mirror mounted on the wall behind Smith. His glance lingered and he appeared to examine it carefully. He noted the opaque cloud that now covered most of the upper third of the mirror.

"Looks like some kind of smear has formed," he said.

"Be sure someone cleans it," Smith instructed Stepanski.

"Can I suggest something?"

"Carry on."

"I think what's happened is that steam from the coffee maker on the shelf there near the door has gotten in between the mirror and the silver. You're not going to get rid of it by rubbing the outside. To do it right, we should take the mirror down and clean the inside. Then you should move the coffee maker."

"How long will that take?"

"About thirty seconds. You just unplug it, find another outlet a little farther away, and there you are."

"I mean the mirror, Stepanski."

"Sure. The mirror. Well, if we can get it down yet today, I don't see any reason why we can't have it cleaned and back up by the close of work detail tomorrow afternoon."

"Do it."

"Yessir."

"And Stepanski—one more thing."

"Yessir."

"Make damn good and sure you protect that mirror properly if it's gonna be in the Supply Room overnight. There's caustics and paint and cleanser and God knows what all else down there, and I do not, repeat, do not want this thing coming back looking worse than it is now."

"Yessir."

* * *

27

Squires went into the kitchen. He leaned against the counter and breathed shallowly, in and out. He looked over at the door. He took a palm-sized fragment of tile out of his pocket and examined it. It looked like the piece for Oklahoma on a puzzle map of the United States. The panhandle was a bit elongated and came to an emphatic point. He tested the point and the edge. They were satisfyingly sharp. He wrapped the fragment in his handkerchief and put it carefully in the breast pocket of his shirt.

Banich went down the back stairs to the basement. He was mildly surprised to see Stepanski and Lanier lugging a six-foot long, three-foot wide mirror and frame down the corridor. At Stepanski's instruction, he put down his own things and fished the hard plastic, computer hole-punched card from Stepanski's shirt pocket. He inserted the card into a slot on the box mounted above the handle on the Supply Room door, waited for the distinctive click, and opened the door.

Stepanski and Lanier carried the mirror into the room and over to the far corner, diagonally across from the door. They set it upright. Stepanski looked over the shelves of miscellaneous supplies and equipment. He examined a sheet and rejected it as too dirty. Then he shook open a large, cream-colored tarpaulin. He looked at both sides, nodded, and threw the tarp over the mirror and frame. It was more than large enough for the purpose, covering the awkward equipment and falling in generous folds at its base.

"You know something?" Stepanski asked the other two as he completed this task. "CO-2 Smith is dumber than a box of rocks."

*C*HAPTER 5

It was with a sense of exhilaration that, from his modest office at the Brookings Institution, Michaelson called the direct dial number of M. Jerome Casper, Counsel for Hemispheric Affairs in the State Department's Office of Legal Advisor. He was very good at the centerpiece tasks expected of foreign service officers: observation, analysis, reporting. He enjoyed them. What he really loved, however, and what he had really missed since his retirement, was operations: making things happen, getting the treaty signed, talking the drunken and obnoxious American businessman out of jail, engineering transfers for excessively uncongenial CIA station chiefs.

That was what he was doing now. He found himself grateful to Wendy Gardner for giving him a concrete problem he could really get his teeth into again.

He reached a secretary who said that Mr. Casper was engaged and asked if she could have him return Mr. Michaelson's call. Michaelson said that she could.

Mr. Casper was in fact not engaged in anything more demanding than skimming a summary of a dense report on the Commerce Department's chronic inability to grasp the relationship between foreign trade and foreign policy. He had his calls screened because if you don't have your calls screened in Washington you never do anything but talk on the phone.

When he saw the neat little pink slip with Michaelson's message on it, and imagined the phone log on his secretary's desk documenting the call for bureaucratic eternity, his own acutely sensitive antennae quivered.

It would be unjust to M. Jerome Casper to suggest that he wouldn't have returned Michaelson's call had Michaelson been just an ordinary citizen. (Of course if Michaelson had been just an ordinary citizen there probably wouldn't have been a call for Casper to return, because an ordinary citizen wouldn't have known Casper's direct dial number or for that matter the fact that Casper or his title existed.) Had such a hypothetical citizen overcome these barriers and called Casper, however, Casper would probably have returned the call, or at least had it returned by somebody else. It might have taken him two or three days to get around to it, but it would've happened.

And it would be equally unjust to M. Jerome Casper to suggest that, had Michaelson been merely a State Department alumnus with whom Casper had been on a first-name basis, he would have greeted the message with only slightly less indifference. In that case, he probably would have called Michaelson back the next morning.

What moved Michaelson higher on Casper's priority list was Casper's knowledge that Michaelson was angling ferociously for a major appointment in the next administration, with at least a ten percent chance that he'd get it. There was a small but real possibility—or risk—that in the foreseeable future he'd be working for Michaelson. He returned Michaelson's call within five minutes.

"Jerry," Michaelson said when Casper came on the line. "Thank you so much for calling back."

"Happy to do it, Dick," Casper said. "What can I do for you?"

"Blaze a trail. I have a call in to a chap at Justice who according to the directory for that department has responsibilities in the white collar crime area. I'm going to try to see him to talk over a problem involving former Senator Gardner."

"What's Gardner's problem, apart from being a guest of the taxpayers?"

"I don't really know yet. I'm supposed to find that out from Gardner tomorrow morning."

"The lawyer at Justice is being difficult?"

"I haven't talked to him yet. I'm assuming that an appointment to see him won't be a problem. But I need to come out of that meeting with more than a handshake and ten minutes of generalities, and it occurs to me that since he has no idea who I am he might be a bit tight-lipped."

"I doubt he has any idea who I am either. I'm not sure I'm the best trailblazer for your purposes."

"Don't underestimate yourself," Michaelson said. "I would find it very useful if you could see your way clear to calling the Assistant Attorney General in charge of the Criminal Division to tell him how harmless and patriotic I am."

"Can I just conceal material information or do I have to out-and-out lie?" Casper chuckled.

"Use your own judgment," Michaelson answered, politely returning the chuckle.

"You know," Casper said then, "that proposal to turn all responsibility for drug interdiction over to a single super agency that would take over for the FBI, the INS, the DEA and two or three other outfits has reared its head again."

"I think I did read something about that in the *Post* a week or so ago."

"DOJ"—bureaucratese for the Department of Justice— "is very anxious not to get dealt out of the action on that."

"I can imagine."

"Because of the role Colombia and some other Latin American countries play in the drug-smuggling problems, DOJ has the idea that my office's opinion on the super agency plan could have considerable influence."

"I suspect they're right about that, don't you?" Michaelson asked.

"The thing is," Casper said, "if I call the Assistant Attorney General in charge of the Criminal Division, with both of us knowing how anxious he is for me to make helpful noises on this super agency idea, he might think that I was trying to extract a favor for you in exchange for adopting DOJ's line on the drug thing."

"I doubt that he has such a devious turn of mind. In any event, I'm sure you'll make it clear to him that there's no connection whatever between the two matters."

"Tell me, Dick, if I said that to him—there's no connection, et cetera—do you think that might only tend to emphasize the very possibility of such a connection?"

"You may well be right," Michaelson commented. "Perhaps it's better not to mention it at all."

There was silence on the line for about three seconds. Casper thought it over. Ten percent at least.

"What's your time frame for this meeting?" Casper asked finally.

"Early Friday morning, day after tomorrow," Michaelson said crisply. "Thank you, Jerry."

Wendy Gardner stuck with her assignment for almost forty-five minutes after she got to the Library of Congress. Then, two things happened almost simultaneously. First, she began to realize how unspeakably tedious it was going to be to keep paging through dusty reports for the three or four hours it would take to compile the information Michaelson had asked for. Second, she came as if providentially across Randy Cox's name.

Cox had been one of her father's key aides, going clear back to when she still lived in Washington. She had known him pretty well. He was one of the people she was supposed to put on her list for Michaelson. So she checked the Congressional Staff Directory to see where he had gone once her father no longer had a staff for him to be on. And she found that he had gone on to the staff of the Subcommittee on Western Hemisphere Trade of the Senate International Commerce Committee.

So that was simple, she told herself. No need to plow through a stack of dreary documents from the Government Printing Office. All she had to do was hike a single marble block to the Dirksen Building and have a talk with Randy.

The interiors of congressional office buildings all present the same rather striking contrast. The public areas—hallways, corridors, hearing rooms—are so richly appointed and so far beyond human scale as to seem inappropriate for what is after all a republic. If you penetrate into actual working space, such as staff offices, on the other hand, this impression of opulence vanishes. There you see the people who actually write the first drafts of the nation's laws laboring at unadorned, gray metal desks, squeezed in between bulging file cabinets, buried under mounds of green-covered hearing records, staple-bound reports, and untidy typescript.

Wendy felt at home in these precincts. She had visited them often while she lived in Washington, and less often but still not infrequently during the years between her exile back to the midwest and her father's conviction. She found the office of the subcommittee staff without difficulty and asked the first harried secretary she came to—the staff didn't have a receptionist—if she could see Randy Cox.

The secretary wasn't at all sure she could and seemed in no particular hurry to find out. Cox short-circuited the rather promising confrontation by recognizing Wendy from across the room.

"I'll be with you as soon as I kill an amendment," he bellowed.

Cox disappeared for a moment behind three stacks of papers tottering precariously on the front edge of a desk. He bobbed back up, dropped a printed page with KILL written across it into a wire basket, and strode across the room. Shaking Wendy's hand warmly, he escorted her toward the tiny cubicle alotted to him.

Cox was in his mid-thirties. Wendy realized that during much of the time he had served her father he must have been about as young as the wonks she'd seen listening to Michaelson that morning. He had seemed much older to her—but of course she'd been younger then herself. Cox had dark, flat hair that he wore just barely long enough to comb. His face was smooth, round and tan. He was about four inches taller than she was, and about sixty pounds heavier. She remembered him as always having his suit coat off with his tie loosened and the top button on his shirt unfastened, and he looked the same way now.

They reached his desk, separated by a shoulder-high, aluminum and particle board partition from desks on either side. Motioning her toward a chair, he circled behind the desk, sat down, joined his hands behind his head, and put his feet on the desk over a massive clutter of paper.

"So," he said, "how's the senator handling it?"

"As well as could be expected, I suppose."

"He should be getting out soon, shouldn't he?"

"We're hoping."

"Just hoping? Is there trouble?"

"There may be," Wendy allowed. "It's really too early to tell."

"Anything I can do to help?"

"Well, actually—"

"You knew he got me this job, didn't you?" Cox interjected. "He took care of everyone on his staff. When he knew he was in trouble and there wasn't any way out, he made sure all his staffers had something else to go to."

"I didn't actually know that. It doesn't surprise me, though. Listen, you asked if there was anything you could do to help."

"Right. Anything."

34

"I need some information."

"Uh, information. You mean like Committee information?"

"Yes, committee information."

"Um, well, yes. That is, ah, Wendy, you realize that much of the information that, uh, comes to the Committee is very, ah, sensitive, and—"

"Excuse me?" Wendy said sharply, her eyes flaring at Cox's indecently hasty retreat from his promise to do anything he could to help.

"Well, Wendy, you said you want Committee information and I can't just hand out Committee information to everyone who'd like to have it."

"Randy, I want information *about* committees."

"I'm sorry. Maybe I spoke too quickly. What specifically do you need?"

Wendy told him.

"Oh," Cox said. "That I can do. I thought you were looking for something else."

Cox swung his feet off his desk, sat upright behind it and picked up his phone. He punched three buttons and then spoke into it.

"Listen, Cheryl, I need rosters, last six years, this subcommittee and the same one on the House side, members and members' staffs and subcommittee staffs. . . . Yes, Cheryl, I know you're working on something right now. You're working on a bodice ripper and a Virginia Slim. So why don't you just get up off your lazy butt and get me the goddamn rosters, because I need 'em, okay?"

Wendy could readily imagine that the vehemence with which Cox slammed the receiver down wasn't just irritation affected for her benefit. The power that Cox and people like him enjoy comes at a price. A twenty-four-year-old kid fresh out of law school could go to any firm on Connecticut Avenue and get twice what Cox was making and a secretary who'd do what she was told without talking back.

35

"What did you think I was asking for?" Wendy asked.

"I don't know," Cox said, shrugging. "You know."

Wendy didn't know.

"There's lots of confidential stuff around here," Cox said. "We've got estimates of Chilean copper production for the next twelve months, computer projections of next season's Peruvian cocoa yield and fourteen other things that the average futures market broker would sell his mother to get. We have to be careful."

"Oh."

"What's the senator need the rosters for?"

"I'm not sure," Wendy answered. "Actually, he wasn't the one who asked me to get them. It was somebody else."

"Who, if you don't mind my asking?"

"You don't know him. An old guy from State named Michaelson that dad asked me to get in touch with."

"Not Richard Michaelson?"

"Yeah, that's the one."

"Okay," Cox said, looking away.

Cheryl came in at this point and ungently dumped a half inch of paper in front of Cox. In apparent defiance of Newton's Second Law of Motion, she seemed to begin moving away from Cox's desk the same instant, without ever having reached a full stop during her journey toward the desk.

"Hey, Cheryl," Cox called to her as he thumbed the papers.

"Yeah?" She half-turned and looked over her shoulder at him.

"The law against sex discrimination doesn't apply to Congress. Did you know that, Cheryl?"

"What—"

"And the Civil Service Act doesn't apply to Congress either. Did you know that?"

"*You* wanna know something, Randy?" Cheryl said, turning around to face him and displaying complete indifference to the information that she could be fired at will without any recourse. "You've got a real elitist attitude."

Cox paused for one beat. He smiled. Then he said, "Watch your mouth, peasant."

Cheryl walked away quickly. She was stifling either a laugh or a scream and Wendy couldn't tell which.

"What did you mean when you made that remark about Richard Michaelson?" Wendy asked after Cheryl had disappeared. "When you said o-*kay* like that, like ohhhh-*kay* and got this look on your face like I'd just ordered Vichyssoise at McDonalds. What'd all that mean?"

"Wendy, all I can tell you is that that guy's got his own agenda."

"Meaning what?"

"He has a definite idea about where he wants to be when the next President comes in, and it's not in the private sector. He'd lie, cheat or steal to get on the right guy's short list for one of the jobs he has in mind."

Wendy shrugged. What Cox was saying so far tallied pretty well with what Michaelson had told her himself.

"So what?" she said.

"So keep your eyes open. He'd walk over the Senator to get where he wants to go. He'd sure as hell walk over you. Watch your back. And if there's anytime you feel like giving me a call and asking about what he's doing, don't think twice about it, okay? Just do it. Okay?" He wrote two phone numbers on the top page of the papers he was about to give her.

"Okay. I guess."

"Look. Can I call you? I mean if I shake myself free from here long enough for dinner or something?"

Wendy thought about that for a second.

"Maybe," she said then, smiling. Her smile was enchanting when she wanted it to be. It was enchanting now. But she didn't give him her phone number at Hartnett Hall. "I'll give you a call later on and we'll talk about it."

37

*   *   *

Michaelson walked into Cavalier Books around 5:30. He picked up a copy of *L'Expres* from the periodicals rack in the front and wandered back among the bookshelves. He found his own book, three copies displayed spine out.

He took one down and glanced at the cover and the back flap. He nodded as if impressed with the subtle wisdom that the jacket copy promised. He paged through the slim volume and nodded again, as if the bits he read clearly fulfilled this promise. His expression as he reached up to replace the book was absent, suggesting that he was still preoccupied with the thought-provoking profundities he had serendipitously discovered. By the time he was through replacing the book it was displayed face out, with the full front of the cover showing.

He made his way toward the other side of the store where you could walk up three wooden steps to a small platform, buy a cup of coffee or tea, and sit at one of two tiny tables.

This addition to the booksellers' trade had been popular in Washington for several years, and it was Michaelson's observation that it worked. That is, it drew to the bookstore in the evening people who came not to buy books but to meet other people, generally of gender opposite to their own, and who more than occasionally ended up buying books as a by-product of this activity. So much nicer, Michaelson imagined, to tell your mother that you'd met the boy at a bookstore than to say you'd run into each other at a bar.

He had just about finished an article on the future of proportional representation in the French National Assembly when he spotted Marjorie Randolph mounting the steps to join him. He stood up and held out the other chair at the table where he was sitting.

"Good evening, Marjorie. May I buy you a cup of your coffee?"

"You may buy me a cup of my tea, thank you," she said, Virginia tidewater washing gently through her voice. Marjorie sat down and fetchingly shook the chestnut hair that, naturally or chemically, still offered no hint of gray after forty-seven years.

Michaelson signaled to the counter and sat back down.

"I've restored your book to its original display, by the way," she said.

"Ah. You noticed."

"Yes, I noticed. Richard, I *do* wish you wouldn't do that."

"You're quite right. I'm very sorry."

"It is my store, after all."

"Marjorie, you are absolutely correct. It was a mischievous impulse that I should have tried harder to resist. It was quite wrong of me. I apologize."

"You know, Richard," Marjorie sighed, "you can be quite charming when you choose to be."

"You're not too surprised, are you? For thirty-five years I was essentially paid to be charming when I chose to be."

"We actually sold a copy of your book today, if you can believe it. And to a real person. Not a campaign staffer."

"Yes, as it happens I did know that." Michaelson examined a long, nearly invisible strand of blond hair that he'd picked up while rearranging the display of his book. "Off hand, I'd say you sold it late this morning to a blond-haired young woman of medium height and weight, fair complexion, blue eyes and a disarmingly direct type of approach."

"Richard," Marjorie said, "that was positively Sherlockian. How in the world did you figure all that out from a single hair?"

"I didn't, to tell the truth. I met her earlier today. A bit before noon she came into a meeting I was involved in. She had a copy of the book which in the course of the meeting she took out of a sack from this store. That much was observation. The rest was simple logic."

"I dare say."

"Her name is Wendy Gardner, by the way. Senator Gardner's daughter."

39

"That's it," Marjorie said, snapping her fingers silently. "I thought the name rang a bell."

"I know Senator Gardner very well. He and I go back quite a way. But I don't think I ever got to know anyone in his family."

"It's a fairly standard Washington story, I'm afraid," Marjorie commented. "Things were more or less all right until Wendy got to be about thirteen. There were the occasional infidelities in the back seats of limos at embassy parties and that kind of sordid nonsense, but nothing really fundamentally wrong, if you understand me."

"I do."

"Then Wendy's mother decided that Wendy was turning into your basic D.C. brat, running with friends who were too rich, too fast and too sophisticated, getting away from where she came from and so forth, becoming more D.C. than midwest."

"Did Wendy's mother react in the customary way?"

"Naturally. She jerked the little jewel back to live with her in cow country, in the house they maintained in the home state for official residency purposes. The rest was the way it usually is."

"Divorce?" Michaelson asked.

"Within two years. Eight months later, he remarried."

"Someone on the staff?"

"Of course."

"Yes, you did say the way it usually is."

"It was less than three years after the remarriage that they videotaped him with his paw in the cookie jar."

"That part I knew."

"The proverbial prison door had slammed behind him about fifteen minutes before the second honey served her own set of divorce papers."

"A Washington tragedy."

"The only one it's tragic for is Wendy," Marjorie said. "The rest of them got what was coming to them."

———

Marjorie looked with undisguised malice at a plastic sign hanging over the tea-and-coffee bar. It showed a lighted cigarette with a red circle around it and a red slash through the circle.

"It says something about the bureaucratic mind, don't you think, that I should be required to put a non-verbal sign up to communicate a message as simple as No Smoking in a bookstore? You'd think that anyone coming into a bookstore would have enough English to handle that much. Wouldn't you?"

"I haven't a doubt."

"I have suggested to my lawyer that it is unconstitutional for the District of Columbia City Council to forbid me to smoke in my own establishment. It's bad enough that they won't let me serve wine here. I've instructed her not to call me back until she has a satisfactory answer."

"Good luck."

"Until now," Marjorie said wistfully, "the only institution I've ever been associated with where I was forbidden the consolations of both alcohol and tobacco was the Amelia Fairfax Academy for Young Ladies—and that's the only place where I ever partook immoderately of either."

"Well," Michaelson said sympathetically, "smoking is permitted in my apartment, and wine has been known to be available."

"What else is on the menu?"

"Oh, I don't know. Baloney sandwiches. Carry-out pizza. Whatever."

"You have yourself a date, Richard. I'll give Carrie the keys so she can lock up."

41

CHAPTER 6

SECURE PERIMETER AHEAD
REDUCE SPEED TO 15 MPH

"Do you suppose they mean a fence?" Michaelson asked, glancing at the white-on-green metal sign.

"They mean it about slowing down," Wendy said. "There're speed bumps just after this curve coming up."

"Then we shall certainly obey."

Michaelson braked the eight-year-old Dodge Omni Hatchback he was driving and downshifted.

They saw the chain-link fence topped with razor wire fifteen yards beyond the last speed bump. A free-standing sign said in raised silver-gray letters on a pebbled blue background that they were about to enter the Federal Minimum Security Correctional Facility (Fritchieburg).

The principal gate was open, the breach guarded only by a black-and-yellow striped barricade arm. They stopped before the plywood arm long enough to be scrutinized by a man inside a tinted-glass sentry box and to read a sign commanding them peremptorily to park at the first available space past the gate and proceed immediately to the Guard House.

The barrier swung upward. Michaelson drove the Omni forward and parked it between two orange lines in a grease-stained, paved enclosure perhaps fifty yards square. They got out and walked to a featureless, one-story building opposite the gate. Inside this structure they showed their drivers' licenses to a steely-eyed young woman in a light-brown-with-loden-green-trim uniform, said why they had come, and signed a register. In exchange for their signatures they received plastic-encased badges marked VISITOR (B-4).

Wendy laid her purse on a long, scarred table. They both stepped through a metal detector. A second guard dumped the contents of Wendy's purse unceremoniously on the table and briefly sorted through its contents.

"You'll have to leave the cigarettes and the lighter here," he told her. He handed her a white matchbook stamped in smeared, blue ink with the seal of the Department of Justice undergirded by the words Federal Bureau of Prisons. "There's a cigarette machine and a dollar bill changer in the waiting room."

Wendy and Michaelson proceeded to the latter area, which took up the rear third of the Guard House. They were the only ones there. A large sign informed them that visitors were to wait for shuttles to take them to the buildings indicated on their badges, and were not to leave those buildings except in the company of security personnel.

"And this is *minimum* security," Wendy said.

"It's considerably more secure than any embassy I ever served in," Michaelson agreed.

"The natives were probably friendlier."

"Don't be too sure."

Ten minutes later a small schoolbus painted olive drab pulled up outside the Guard House lobby. Wendy and Michaelson got on and showed the driver their visitors' badges. The bus chugged away from the Guard House, passed a long, boxy, four-floor building with a sign reading ADMINISTRATION in front and drove them through a succession of curves and Y forks to a waist-high cyclone fence demarcating sector B. Landscaped hillocks and the twists of the prison roadway isolated it from the Guard House and Administration Building a few hundred yards away.

"You'll have one minute to get through the gate once I punch in the code," the driver told them. "B-4 is the last building to your right."

Michaelson and Wendy climbed off the bus and heard a metallic thunk just after the driver punched four buttons on a key pad mounted near the gate. They pushed the gate open and went through.

Cottages B-1, B-2 and B-3 were grouped together, near the gate, no more than ten yards separating one from the other. Honor Cottage B-4 was a good one hundred-fifty yards away from them, separated not only by a wide swatch of beaten earth but by a six-hoop, concrete outdoor basketball court and an asphalt tennis court. Between the two courts and the cottage itself, they could see part of the twelve-foot wide lawn that went around the building—a humanizing embellishment the other buildings in sector B lacked.

They walked up to B-4 and went in the front door. A videocamera hummed and turned its glassy eye toward them. The only doorway opened to their right, channeling them through a modest lobby furnished with shell-shaped chairs made out of dove-gray molded fiberglass and tubular steel. On the other side of this room was another doorway, this one guarded by a metal detector. Correctional Officer Grade-2 Smith had already bounded out of the Building Security Office and was waiting for them on the opposite side of the metal detector.

Wendy passed through the device without incident. Michaelson stepped confidently through and was startled when a harsh beep sounded, accompanied by a rasping buzz from the Building Security Office.

"Must have some metal on you," Smith said as he flipped a switch to cut off the alarms.

"I don't think so," Michaelson muttered, genuinely puzzled. "The detector at the Guard House didn't go off."

"I crank the ones I'm in charge of up a couple of clicks," Smith said.

Michaelson's belt buckle was leather and his car keys and loose change rested in a plastic tray beside the protesting device. He patted the pockets of his sport coat, felt something underneath the lining of the breast pocket, and sheepishly fished it out. It was a nail clipper, smaller than Wendy's little finger. He dropped this into the plastic tray and passed again through the metal detector while Smith nodded knowingly.

"We're here to visit Desmond Gardner," Wendy told the guard.

"Room 104," Smith said. "Straight down the ground floor corridor, on your left. Inmate Gardner is permitted to receive visitors in his room, in common areas, such as the lounge on the ground floor, and on the grassy area immediately surrounding this building. Don't go anywhere else. Carry on."

Smith went back into his office.

Their footsteps echoed hollowly as they walked down the corridor. Alternating red and white squares of vinyl tile covered a bare concrete floor that showed through in spots. There was no carpeting. Another video camera gazed down the length of the hall, and Wendy imagined expressionless people in light-brown-and-loden-green uniforms watching her on a TV screen somewhere as she tramped down the brightly lit passageway.

"To tell you the truth," Michaelson said, "it reminds me of the graduate center dormitories at Harvard—except that we had to walk a lot farther to play tennis."

They paused in front of a wooden door marked 104. Wendy hesitated for a moment, glanced at Michaelson, then raised her hand and knocked tentatively. The sound of two or three steps came from inside and then the door swung open.

"Wendy!" Desmond Gardner exclaimed, surprise and delight lighting up his voice. He and his daughter hugged each other tightly.

"I brought someone to see you," Wendy panted when they had broken the clinch and she had gotten a chance to catch her breath.

"So you did," Gardner said, glancing up in slight em-

45

barrassment at Michaelson. "I'm very glad to see you, Dick." He reached out and shook Michaelson's hand. "Sorry about ignoring you for a moment there. I asked Wendy when we talked Sunday to get in touch with you, but I had no idea she'd manage to get you out here so soon, and I certainly wasn't anticipating that she'd be able to come along with you."

"I didn't expect to get out here so fast myself," Wendy said. "I didn't get a chance to phone yesterday until it was too late to get a call through."

"Good to see you again, Senator," Michaelson said.

Gardner stepped back from the doorway so that Wendy and Michaelson could move into his nine by nine foot room.

"I wish it could have been under different circumstances," Gardner said. "But that's the way it is. We are where we are."

Michaelson glanced around. The room combined the depressing and the pathetic. The walls were peach-painted cinderblock. One bed, one wardrobe, one table and one chair, all made of cheap wood. A small television and a clock radio sat on the table near a current Almanac of American Politics and a U.S. Statistical Abstract. The front section of yesterday's *Washington Post* lay beside the chair. A deck of cards rested on top of the radio. On the walls Gardner had taped a handful of framed mementoes from the career that his greed had blasted: a black-and-white picture of Gardner looking over President Reagan's shoulder while the President signed a bill; a certificate from the National Rifle Association congratulating him on qualifying as a Marksman (Handgun); a yellowed scrap of newsprint with the headline, Gardner Upsets Prescott. There were no other books, no chessboard, not even a pad and pen.

"Well," Michaelson said, clasping his hands behind his back and turning toward Gardner. "Why don't you tell me what it is you think I might be able to help you with?"

Gardner sat down on the bed and put both hands behind him to brace himself.

"Did Wendy give you the broad outlines?" he asked.

"Yes. She said that the U.S. Attorney from your state is

threatening to try to block your parole unless you give him information that you don't have. He won't tell you what the information is, except for a broad hint that it relates in some way to sugar and alleged corruption."

"That's it in a nutshell."

"Do you have any idea what he was talking about?"

"None. And I don't think he does either."

"What do you think he was doing?" Michaelson asked.

"Fishing."

"He must've had some hint that there was something to catch."

"You're right," Gardner agreed. "He must have. But I don't have the first notion of what it could be."

"You were on the Western Hemisphere Trade Subcommittee, which if I remember correctly does deal with sugar import quotas every year."

"You're damn right I was. I had a soft drink bottling plant and a major candy company in my state. If I'd let those crackers from Louisiana have their way every year, there wouldn't be any sugar imports, the price of sugar would go through the roof, and seventeen thousand registered voters would be very upset with me. I had to pay attention to what went on on that subcommittee."

"Just so. Was it really that bad—setting the import quotas, I mean?"

"It was as bad as you could possibly imagine," Gardner assured him. "An annual bloodletting. A regular Washington orgy of hustling and lobbying and logrolling."

"Did you see any evidence of outright corruption—bribery, that kind of thing—in the process?"

Gardner stood up abruptly and folded his arms across his chest. He looked away from Michaelson, expelling his breath in a long sigh. He walked over to the table and leaned against it.

"Let me tell you a story," he said.

"All right."

47

"The year before my last election, the lobbyist for the National Association of Nursing Professionals made an appointment and came to see me. She asked me if I was familiar with Carepac. That was her association's political action committee. I said that I was."

"Yes?" Michaelson prompted.

"Then she asked me what my position was on a bill that would reduce federal aid to hospitals that filled administrative positions with nurses who came from diploma schools instead of limiting them to nurses who'd gotten bachelor's degrees from four-year schools."

"I take it that this question was pregnant with implication."

"That's putting it mildly. I didn't give a tinker's dam whether that bill passed or failed or never came to a vote. On my list of twenty things to worry about, it was around fifty-third. The lobbyist knew that. But I knew that Carepac was giving campaign contributions to senators who were willing to support the bill. I knew that no one was giving campaign contributions to senators who opposed the bill. The lobbyist knew that I knew these things."

"You're suggesting that the outcome of your deliberations on the merits of this measure was foreordained."

"Exactly. I told her I was a fervent believer in professionalizing the nurses' calling and that I would therefore support the bill. The next week, my campaign committee received a check."

"Thus illustrating—what, precisely?"

"You see, Dick, *that* wasn't a bribe. That's not the kind of thing I got sent to prison for. *That* was democracy in action. *That* was business as usual."

"I do see, yes."

"That kind of thing was absolutely par for the course when the annual sugar import quotas were set. No one made any bones about it. That's what I know about. I could give them chapter and verse on that until they were tired of listening to me."

"But, if I catch your meaning, that couldn't be what they're interested in, because it's open, notorious and apparently legal.

"It's even subtler than that," Gardner insisted. "How could they be looking for anything? How could there be anything for them to look for? How can you possibly *have* corruption when you have political action committees? What's the point? Why bribe someone under the table when you can bid for his vote on the open market?"

"That's a persuasive if depressingly cynical observation."

"I don't mean it to sound cynical. I'm just saying if there was some importer that felt he had to buy some votes, and some senators who were capable of being bought, no one had to pass around hundred dollar bills in white envelopes. You just get the right PAC man to drop the right hint. Everyone knows that the sugar quotas get set in a sixteen-hour marathon committee session where everybody gives something and everybody takes something and there's no way in the world to say any particular quota should've been a couple of hundred tons more or a couple of hundred less. Bribery would be superfluous."

"So your conclusion is that the U.S. Attorney's office back home was just taking a shot in the dark. They assumed that there must be something, and they hoped that you could be pressured or bluffed into providing a lead they could work with, even though they really had no specific notion of what they were looking for."

"That's right."

"Well," Michaelson said, "it's not a theory I'd reject out of hand. I'll make some phone calls and see what I can find out. If it's just a self-important political hack trying to make mischief, I should be able to track down someone who can sort it out."

"I appreciate that, Dick. I really do."

"I'm happy to do it."

"There's something else," Gardner said then.

"Yes. Wendy said that you thought you might be at risk in some way. Physical risk."

"That's right. I—" Gardner stopped abruptly and began striding toward the door. "Look. Do you mind if we get out of here for a bit, go out and talk on the lawn?"

"Lead the way," Michaelson said.

"I know what you're thinking," Gardner said, glancing over his shoulder as he stepped through his door. "This isn't a prison, it's a country club, and it's a little bit priggish to act claustrophobic about it."

"Not—" Michaelson began.

"I don't blame you. All I can say is, I don't care what it looks like from the outside, it's still a prison. It's not a country club. If I get turned down for parole in two months, I have to wait at least six months before I can be considered again. The thought of spending that much more time in here makes me feel like there's something very unpleasant crawling around my insides."

CHAPTER 7

There were two ways out of the building from Gardner's room. Gardner chose the one that didn't go past the Building Security Office, with its succession of bottlenecks and the petty aggravation of CO-2 Smith's personal scrutiny.

He led them to the basement and then, just past the Supply Room, down an intersecting hallway that led to an outside door. They walked up metal steps to the lawn. Gardner's pace slowed at this point, and they proceeded at a sedate stroll around the back of the building to the other side.

"Generally speaking, you get a particular kind of inmate in a place like this, particular kinds of crimes," Gardner said. He pointed out Squires and Lanier playing tennis. "Take those two guys for example."

"I'd say that they don't exactly look like burglars, but I don't really know what burglars look like," Michaelson said.

"They're not burglars, that's for sure. Squires was a lawyer. He signed on with a big firm and two years later they'd told him to take a hike, because he's not a can do kind of guy. So, he opened his own shop, scrapped around, and one fine day a new client called him. The client said he had this little problem with some money he was a little nervous about. Could Squires solve this problem? Can do, said Squires, who'd learned his lesson. Now he's doing time. You see what I'm driving at?"

"No," Michaelson said.

"Or take Lanier. Lanier was a computer software designer and programmer. It was the perfect job for him. He's basically a propeller head who'd love to spend twenty hours a day playing with a keyboard, and he found a company that'd not only let him do that but paid him for it. Unfortunately for him, he got a dream."

"It must have been an expensive dream," Michaelson commented.

"In more ways than one. He thought he'd figured out how to write a program that would translate the human voice directly into type. You know, you dictate into one end and a memo comes out the other."

"It sounds like the kind of thing that could put his children through college all right," Michaelson said.

"Problem was, he needed about two million dollars to go from concept to prototype. He couldn't interest anyone else, so one night he cranked up his Hewlett Packard, infiltrated a ledger six states away, and authorized himself his own little R & D budget. He ran through about six hundred thousand dollars before he got caught, and all he had to show for it was a lot of chips and circuit boards that didn't have a hell of a lot of other applications. The judge said he could have three years to think things over."

"All right," Michaelson said.

"Then we have Stepanski," Gardner remarked, nodding toward a muscular, smiling, curly-haired man playing basketball with Banich. "He and his twin brother and their little brother all went to Nam together. They stuck together and came through okay. Back in New Orleans they started a little construction business.

"Then someone passed the word that a certain percentage of the city and parish construction projects have to go to minority-owned businesses. Larry Stepanski set up his janitor, who's black, with his own construction company on paper. That company got its share of the minority set asides. It subcontracted the work to Stepanski Construction. Everyone got a cut. Everyone was happy."

"I had no idea that kind of thing was a federal crime," Michaelson said.

"It's not a crime, it's a loophole. Everyone knew exactly what was going on. The local officials had nice minority business numbers to send to Washington. The bureaucrats in Washington had nice results to report to Congress when appropriation time came."

"Then why is Mr. Stepanski in prison?"

"Time passed. Stepanski's twin brother died. Of AIDS. Stepanski hadn't had any idea. He was totally devastated and basically went on a six-month drunk. Meanwhile, interest rates skyrocketed and the baby brother was in over his head. By the time Stepanski pulled himself together, the company needed a lot of cash fast and the only plausible source was a loan shark.

"That left the problem of paying off the loan shark. Then Stepanski heard that his progressive federal government was willing to make loans to minority business enterprises. Stepanski trotted out the janitor, got a loan, and was just about to pay off the shylock when the federal authorities found out what was going on and Stepanski learned that this wasn't quite the same thing as helping local officials massage their community development statistics."

"So Mr. Stepanski went to prison for attempting to defraud his government?"

"Right. Then there's Banich. He'd been hustling, promoting, looking for a big break all his life. Then one day, some product idea fell in his lap. He was certain he had the next IBM, Xerox and Apple Computer rolled into one. All he needed was a little venture capital, but he couldn't find any capitalists quite that venturesome. So he went to a bank and fudged things a bit on his net worth statement. Unfortunately for him, the bank was insured by the FDIC. If the idea had gone over like he thought it would—sincerely thought it would, now—then he would've paid back the bank and no one'd care

---

about the lies on the net worth statement. But the idea didn't go over and the bank took a hit and Mr. Banich has to serve time behind bars."

"Who's the gentleman over there?" Michaelson nodded toward McCutcheon, sitting crosslegged on the grass, looking at but not watching the tennis game.

"His name's Tommy McCutcheon. He's owned a bar in Boston for a long time. One year, he couldn't afford to pay his taxes, so he didn't file a return. For six months he waited for the thunderbolt. Nothing happened. Nine months and nothing happened. Twelve months and nothing happened. So he didn't file a return again. Went on for twenty years. Then, finally, a computer burped and he got nailed."

"You seem to be remarkably conversant with the stories all these men have to tell," Michaelson commented.

"Gift of gab," Gardner nodded. "First quality of a politician. I built a career out of making it easy for people to talk to me. Everybody has a story to tell, and everybody's favorite subject is himself."

"Present company included?" Michaelson asked quietly.

"Excuse me?"

"You have a story to tell, just like all the others. Do you want to tell it to me now?"

Gardner smiled without showing his teeth and shook his head.

"One of the points I wanted to make with this little rundown," he said, "was that not one of these guys believes that he deserves to be here. None of them deny that they're guilty. None of them say that they didn't do what the government indicted them for. But all of them rationalize it. All of them will say, one way or another, that there's so much other stuff that people get away with that's so much worse than anything they did that it just doesn't make any sense for them to be in prison and the other guys to be on the outside."

"And do you feel that way too? About yourself, I mean."

"No," Gardner answered. "I don't rationalize. I've held

onto that much self respect. I committed a crime. I peddled my influence. I betrayed my trust. I compromised my office."

"Nothing's ever quite as simple as that."

"Oh, I could make excuses. It wasn't pure venality. The guy had been paying me $250 to $750 a month for several years. For consulting services. And I consulted whenever he wanted me to. He'd ask a question and I'd answer it, on my own stationery, without using any government staff. All open and aboveboard. Perfectly legitimate."

"But he decided to ask for something more," Wendy said bitterly.

"That he did. He asked me for a mark-up copy of a pending tax bill twenty-four hours before it was supposed to be made public. I knew it was wrong. I knew it was different from what I'd done before. But I also knew I was trapped. I couldn't do without those checks every month."

"So you delivered what he asked," Michaelson said.

"It seemed like such a small thing. I mean, it wasn't like I was selling my vote or anything like that. That's what I told myself. Then I saw Desmond Gardner on that videotape, handing over the big brown envelope with the mark-up bill in it, and getting a little white envelope with his check. I saw that and I realized that I was just as guilty as I could be. I realized I'd really been guilty all those years when I accepted those consulting fees. I was bought and sold without even knowing it. He put me on layaway, and paid for me on the installment plan."

"All right," Wendy said. She said it with some vehemence, and Gardner and Michaelson looked quickly at her. "All right," she repeated, more softly. "But that doesn't mean you should spend one more hour in prison than you ought to just because some lawyer back home thinks you know something you don't know."

"Amen to that," Gardner said smiling.

"I'm going to have to excuse myself in a couple of minutes," Michaelson interjected at that point. "One of the well

---

55

known infirmities of age. But before I do, I'd like to get back to the point we were about to discuss when we adjourned to here from your room. About your being in danger."

"Right," Gardner said. "That was the other point of my little disquisition on what all of my fellow inmates here at Honor Cottage B-4 are doing time for."

"Forgive my dullness," Michaelson said, "but what was that other point exactly?"

"There's one inmate I haven't told you about," Gardner responded. "You see that simian type over there leaning against the backstop on the far side of the tennis court, watching Lanier and Squires play?"

"Yes."

"That's Sweet Tony Martinelli. He comes from Miami."

"And why is Mr. Martinelli in prison?"

"I don't know what the technical legal term is, but when I was in Congress we called it labor racketeering. Had a great ring to it that really played well back home . . . labor racketeering. Martinelli's speciality was persuading union members not to be overly inquisitive about what's happening to their pension funds, and convincing non-union members that it was better not to interfere with illegal work stoppages that got called to shake down employers. He was a thumb breaker. Literally. That was his technique."

"I imagine it was very persuasive indeed."

"Now, I'm sure you've picked out the difference between Martinelli and the rest of us here at the Honor Cottage," Gardner said.

"You mean that you and your fellow inmates are all guilty of white collar crimes—paper crimes, essentially—whereas Mr. Martinelli is a professional perpetrator of violent crimes."

"Right," Gardner confirmed. "Violent crimes traditionally associated with what is politely called organized crime, so as not to abrade the sensibilities of ethnic groups that don't like you to call it the mafia."

"You're suggesting that he's somewhat out of place here."

"You could say that. You might say that if this really were a country club, we would've blackballed him."

"In fact," Michaelson continued, "if I take your point, he is so far out of place here that you suspect his presence must have been procured in irregular fashion and for a reason."

"That, I'm afraid, is exactly right. If the U.S. Attorney back home thinks I must know something about corrupt dealings in sugar quotas, then whoever was doing the dealing must think I know something about it too."

"And that person, you fear, may have arranged for Mr. Martinelli to come here to shut you up."

"That's what I'm afraid of," Gardner admitted. The bantering tone was gone from his voice. When he turned to face Michaelson, the fear showed plainly on his livid features. "I spent enough time in Washington to learn something about organized crime. Those guys aren't as fastidious as the U.S. Attorneys are. They don't fool around with winks and nudges. They just kill you."

CHAPTER 8

"If I retrace the path we took to get here," Michaelson asked, "at what point will I reach the vicinity of a men's room?"

"You can't do it that way," Gardner said. "First, the door we came out of can't be opened from the outside except with a key that I don't have. Second, you have to use the public restroom in the front of the building anyway. Visitors aren't allowed in the inmates' latrine."

"Then I hope you'll excuse me," Michaelson said, and strode purposefully toward the front of Honor Cottage B-4.

"I'm glad he's wandered off for a moment," Wendy said, as soon as Michaelson was out of earshot. "There's something I wanted to ask you."

"So I gathered," Gardner said, smiling. "So did he. That's why he invented that little excursion."

"Was I that obvious?" Wendy asked, blushing as her face softened into a sudden, fetching vulnerabiliity.

"You were transparent, Princess. What's on your mind?"

"Are you sure you can trust him?"

"As sure as you can ever be about anybody. Why?"

"What do you really know about him?"

"I know that he knows the right buttons to push. I know that he can call people all over the senior bureaucracy and get his calls returned. I know that he's willing to help me. What more do I need to know?"

"Why should he be willing to help you?"

"I guess you'd have to ask him to find out for sure. I hoped he'd be willing to help because I did him some favors back when I was still in a position to do favors."

"They must have been pretty big favors."

"They weren't, by Washington standards anyway. But I did at least one of them for—for reasons he particularly approved of. Why don't you tell me what your problem with him is, Wendy?"

"I talked to Randy Cox yesterday," Wendy said then.

"What did Randy have to say?"

"Randy said that Michaelson has his own agenda."

"I certainly hope he does," Gardner snorted. "He wouldn't be much use to me if he didn't."

"I'm not sure I understand."

"Nobody in Washington's going to give you anything just because you're a nice guy with a lot of years of faithful service recorded in your personnel file. If you want something, you have to be in a position to give something in return, now or later. I needed more than somebody with a name from the past. That's why I asked you to contact someone with his own irons in the fire."

Wendy shook her head. "It all seems so—so amorphous somehow. Everything about Washington. There's no solidity to it."

"Smoke and mirrors," Gardner said, nodding, favoring her with a standard-issue, Washington-insider, I-know-things-you-don't-know expression. "That's the nature of the city. Look, I can't come up with some ontological proof that Michaelson's trustworthy. You've just gotta go with your gut on these things."

"I'm not going to just fob you off with a lot of qualitative rhetoric, am I?" Gardner asked.

"I hope not."

"Okay. I first met Dick Michaelson fifteen years ago, when I was still in the House."

"Was this overseas?"

"Yes. I was on a codel."

"Codel?"

"Congressional delegation visit overseas. I guess now that I'm out of Congress for good I should just call them junkets, like other taxpayers do."

"Okay," Wendy said, returning his ironic smile with one of her own that offered no concession. "Tell me about this junket."

"Our subcommittee felt that the national interest imperatively required us to inform ourselves about conditions in Bahrain, which is one Islamic country where you can get a scotch and soda or anything else you want, any time of the day or night. On our way to Bahrain, we passed through the country where Dick was in charge of the U.S. mission. While we were there, things got a little out of hand."

"With the natives or the congressmen?"

"Both, actually, but the immediate concern was the natives. I woke up one morning to find a full-scale riot going on outside the embassy. Huge crowd. Chanting anti-American slogans. Burning the American flag. The whole thing."

"I don't remember that."

"You were four years old, safe and sound at home with your mother. The entire incident only lasted about eighteen hours."

"I bet it seemed like a lot longer to you."

"It sure did," Gardner agreed. "Anyway, as soon as I realized what was going on, I rushed to Dick's office. He was standing at the window, looking out at the crowd, talking on the phone. You have the picture?"

"Mm hmm," Wendy murmured. She enjoyed her father's stories, and she enjoyed the glimpse of the pre-prison Desmond Gardner that shone through when he told one of them.

"Okay. I hurried in. Just as I got there, Dick looked over his shoulder at one of the junior Foreign Service Officers on the embassy staff and said something like, 'Security Condition Two, Mr. So and so.' He said this like he was telling Mr. So and so what the temperature is outside. Well, this junior FSO announced Security Condition Two over an intercom and instantly all hell broke loose. All of a sudden all these guys were rushing all over the embassy, feeding code books into shredders, dumping files into the fireplace and so forth."

"That bad, huh?"

"Bad enough. Congressmen don't get hazardous duty pay. I went over to Dick to see if he could give me a rundown on exactly what was happening. I saw that he'd already been hurt and I got even more nervous. Just as I reached his desk, this big rock hit the window he was looking through. Made an incredible racket. My aide was right behind me, and he grabbed me and pulled me down behind the desk. Guess what Dick did."

"I give up."

"He looked over his shoulder and said, 'That's security glass in the window. It'll take a rocket launcher and a twenty millimeter projectile to shatter it.' So my aide was feeling a little sheepish, lying there on top of me with the window still completely intact and Dick still standing completely unruffled in front of it. So the aide said, 'Suppose they've got something around twenty millimeters out there?' And Dick said, 'In that case, it won't make any difference whether you duck or not.' "

Wendy looked at her father for a long moment.

"And based on that little male bonding experience, you trust him?" she asked, cocking one eyebrow. "I'd say it showed he was brave, cool and arrogant. That's not the same thing as trustworthy."

"What's trustworthy? He gave us the facts without sugarcoating and without melodramatic window dressing. He did it in a situation where he didn't have to and a lot of guys wouldn't have. If you need more than that to trust someone in Washington, then you'll never trust anyone there. Besides, I said that was the first time I met him—not the last time."

"A coy allusion to—what, exactly?"

"I was on the Joint Intelligence Oversight Committee. I got to know Dick pretty well—well enough to believe in him."

"Do you know me well enough to tell me why?" Wendy demanded."

"Sure, but it's the kind of thing that's hard to put into words. It's a feeling that builds up over time, not a logical deduction that you arrive at in a burst of insight." He sighed briefly as he examined his daughter's skeptical and unyielding expression. "Let me give you one more example."

"Okay."

"About five years ago, when Dick had been rotated stateside again, I heard a rumor that a paper in Washington was going to run something embarrassing about one of my aides. Nothing criminal, nothing unethical, nothing involving any wrongdoing, nothing that compromised his efficiency or that anyone had any legitimate interest in knowing. Just a little offbeat taste that the reporter could use to milk a few cheap laughs out of a story on Washington sexual mores."

"And you had Michaelson try to do something about that?"

"As a matter of fact I did."

"What did he do?" Wendy asked, finding herself a little edgy about what the answer might turn out to be.

"He sent me a photocopy of an expense voucher that the reporter had submitted seven years before to the Asian American Press Association to cover the cost of a trip to New Caledonia. He sent along a note that said, 'Never try to buy an American journalist—it's costly enough getting them for free.'"

"I don't get it."

"The Asian American Press Association was a vehicle the CIA used to funnel payments to cooperative journalists. Of course, to make the cover credible, they also had to give some money to reporters who had no idea there was any CIA connection and who thought they were just getting an occupational perk."

"Which category was the repoorter you were worried about in?"

"It didn't make any difference. The CIA wasn't saying and even if it was none of this guy's colleagues would've believed it. If I'd circulated that voucher to half-a-dozen jealous competitors, the reporter would've been stuck with the same kind of unfair, embarrassing story about himself as he was trying to lay on my aide."

"So what happened?"

"I showed the voucher to the reporter and we arrived at an understanding. My aide's name never showed up in print."

"And this makes you *trust* Michaelson?"

"It does."

"Men are incredible."

"I guess we are."

"Let's go back to this embassy riot you were talking about," Wendy said. "You did say Michaelson was hurt when you came in to him the day it happened?"

"Yes. When I got there there was still blood on the sleeve of his coat and one hand was heavily bandaged."

"Mm hmm."

"What's that supposed to mean?"

"Nothing. Look, why don't we talk about something else?"

They talked about something else. They talked about several something elses while minutes slipped by. They didn't notice the tennis game between Squires and Lanier end. They didn't notice Martinelli walk over from where he had been watching, pick up a stray tennis ball, and with unwonted courtesy pop it into the can Lanier held out. They didn't notice the basketball game between Banich and Stepanski conclude. They didn't notice how long Michaelson was taking on what was supposed to have been a trip to the men's room. When Michaelson finally came back, Wendy automatically checked

---

her watch and was astonished to see that it was after eleven o'clock.

"I guess we've been talking a long time," she said, more or less to Michaelson.

"Understandable," Michaelson said. "By the way, there's been a mildly interesting development."

"What's that?"

"The warden of this facility has expressed an interest in giving us a tour of the Administration Building as soon as we're through visiting."

Wendy and her father exchanged glances. Desmond Gardner smiled briefly.

"What does that mean?" Wendy asked Michaelson.

"I don't know. But it seemed to me that the only way to find out was to say yes, so I did."

"When is he expecting us?"

"No particular time. The guard here said that he'll call the warden's office as soon as we leave, and the warden will have us picked up at the sector B gate."

Wendy looked back around at her father.

"I guess we might as well go now," she said. "The sooner we get moving on this problem the feds have created for you, the sooner we'll have it straightened out."

Gardner held out his hand. She took it and they started to shake. Then they fell against each other and hugged.

"You seem preoccupied," Michaelson said to her, after they had been waiting in heavy silence for going on five minutes at the sector B gate.

"I guess I am," she said. She looked away and waited for a moment. Then she added, gesturing with her head toward Honor Cottage B-4, "He trusts you, you know."

"Yes, I do know."

"Why are you helping him?"

"Does it matter?"

"I wouldn't have asked the question if it didn't."

"Excellent point," Michaelson conceded, nodding at her. "I'm helping your father because one time in the course of our careers he had a choice between advancing his own ambitions and doing something that I asked him to do, with nothing but my word to go on as to why he should do it."

"What did you ask him to do?"

"To delay service of a congressional subpoena on a subordinate of mine until he could reach a duty station sufficiently remote that his testimony would have to be taken in writing."

"Why did you ask him to do that?"

"For good and sufficient reason," Michaelson said evenly. "The point is that your father did it, and did it simply because he believed me when I told him that it would be good for America that it be done."

"Listen," Wendy said in a voice suddenly testier and challenging, "do you mind if I ask one thing, as a favor?"

"Not at all."

"Would you mind very much not bullshitting me anymore?"

Michaelson's wince lasted scarcely a second but Wendy caught it.

"I'm sorry if my profanity offends you," she said, her tone scarcely suggesting contrition, "but that's the way women talk these days, and I really would appreciate it if you'd—do what I asked."

"It's vulgarity rather than profanity," Michaelson commented mildly, "inasmuch as it involves no invocation of the Deity or anything held to be sacred, but merely an expression thought in polite society to be indelicate. In all events—"

"I don't believe this," Wendy muttered, crossing her arms across her chest.

"—I wasn't wincing at your use of a barnyard obscenity per se, but at your conversion of a very useful Anglo Saxon noun into a verb. I surmise that what I was doing, in your conception, was either lying to you or feeding you a load of

---

65

bullshit, depending on whether you wished to express yourself concisely or colorfully. The shorthand combination of these two approaches that you resorted to seems to me a compromise that is unhappy from both the grammatical and the rhetorical points of view."

"You are trying to piss me off, aren't you?"

"In what particular, precisely, do you feel I've been less than honest with you?"

Wendy sputtered for a moment in frustration at Michaelson's studied unflappability. She looked away, slapped her palms on the thighs of her jeans, sputtered some more, and finally looked back at him.

"What happened to your little finger?" she demanded, speaking very fast.

"I told you. I lost most of it in an accident."

"You told me all right. What was the accident?"

"My finger was hit by a piece of flying metal."

"Where did the metal come from?"

"It came out of the muzzle of a Kalyshnikov assault rifle," Michaelson said with a smile. "Fortunately, my little finger was the second thing it hit instead of the first."

"Aha! Then why in—*why* did you tell me it was an accident?""

"Because the chap who fired the rifle was aiming at my head."

CHAPTER 9

"From this station," Correctional Officer/Grade 1 Kady said, "we can monitor 112 discrete venues within the compound, up to 6 at any one time."

"Fascinating," Michaelson remarked, glancing at the bank of small television monitors.

"You have a hundred-odd cameras scattered around the prison?" Wendy asked the earnest, uniformed young man.

"The, uh, facility, yes ma'am," Kady said.

"Your escape rate must be minuscule," Michaelson commented. He directed this observation not to Kady but to the older man in mufti whom Kady was nervously trying to impress. The older man's name was F. Whitmore Stevens. The inmates called him Half Whit, an epithet that was as inaccurate as it was inevitable. He was the warden. He had by now spent well over an hour showing Michaelson and Wendy Gardner around the Administration Building and patiently answering their questions.

"Our escape rate is zero," Stevens said. "But the cameras have little to do with that. We don't post them at the perimeter. In a minimum security facility like this, the major security problem isn't unauthorized people getting out but unauthorized material coming in."

"Drugs?"

"Mainly. We deal with that problem by keeping an eye on areas where contraband is most likely to be distributed or used by inmates. A secondary benefit of that approach is that it helps us protect the inmates from each other."

"Is that a big problem?" Wendy asked.

"Fortunately not. And we intend to keep it that way."

"On that point," Michaelson interjected, "it occurs to me that while no one wants to be in prison, if one had to be behind bars one would much rather be here than in most other prisons."

"That's sort of a two-edged comment, but the answer is yes," Stevens acknowledged. "Doing time is unpleasant no matter where you do it. But there are many, many places where it can be a lot more unpleasant than it is here."

"To a layman like myself, that raises an interesting question. Who decides whether a man sentenced to, say, three years for a federal crime is going to serve that time here or in some less congenial place of confinement?"

"It varies," Stevens replied. "Sometimes the sentencing judge. More often the Attorney General."

"Attorney General meaning, functionally, someone in the Bureau of Prisons?"

"Of course."

"On the basis, no doubt, of an array of highly qualitative factors."

"Standard bureaucratic procedure," Stevens nodded.

"But subject, presumably, to specific direction in individual cases from higher up."

"Sure," Stevens shrugged. "It doesn't happen very often, but if the Attorney General or the Assistant Attorney General in charge of the Criminal Division says that Inmate X will be here instead of Leavenworth or Atlanta, here is where he comes."

"Now," Michaelson said, "once X gets here, who decides exactly where X will be lodged? As between, for example, an honor cottage and less privileged quarters?"

"I do," Stevens answered.

"Based on—what?"

"A lot of things. The nature of the offense, the inmate's behavior while in custody, any known past history between this inmate and other inmates here—not to mention institutional considerations ranging from staffing levels to the laundry bill and the season of the year."

"All being further informed by your own sound discretion."

"As a matter of fact, yes. If I've got a funny feeling in my gut about somebody, that can keep him out of an honor cottage even if every objective factor says he belongs in one."

"And once again your decision in this regard is subject to specific direction from your own superiors?"

For the first time since he had introduced himself to them, Stevens hesitated. Though not entirely guileless, he was essentially a straightforward man. Calculation played unambiguously across his features.

"I can't discuss that," he said at last. "At least not without specific direction."

"I can appreciate that," Michaelson commented. "And you would likewise wish to seek official guidance before discussing the assignment of any particular inmate here."

"Correct."

"Recognizing, of course, that if the wrong type of inmate manages to get into an honor cottage, being there might turn out to be not such a great honor for the others."

"We're acutely aware of that."

"I'm sure you are."

"Honor cottages are an incentive—something for an inmate to strive for and try to hang onto if he already has it. They're an extra layer of insulation between a white collar convict and his own worst nightmares about prison. There are certain amenities, but the big attraction is physical and psychological security. We'd defeat the purpose of the honor cottage system if we started putting what you delicately call the wrong type of inmate into honor cottages."

"And as you said the surveillance cameras actually serve to reinforce that sense of security," Michaelson commented.

"That's right," Stevens said. "We locate cameras in places inmates have access to that would otherwise often be out of sight in the ordinary course of things."

"In the latrine, for example, but not in the guards' locker room."

"Right. We can't monitor all locations all the time, but we can monitor any given location at any particular time. The transmissions from each camera are recorded on a continuous, selferasing, eight-minute loop. So if we see something interesting on a random shot, we can go back and pick up what happened up to eight minutes before. The bottom line is, an inmate in a place where we have a camera can't be certain at any given moment that we're not looking right at him."

"Take Honor Cottage B-4, for example," Kady said. "We have six cameras there."

"All inside?" Michaelson asked.

"Yes," Stevens said. "Inside's where trouble's most likely, and outside human eyes are more efficient than electronic ones anyway."

"Anytime we want to," Kady said, "we can punch up any one of the cameras in B-4, or all six of them for that matter."

His fingers moved effortlessly over a keyboard in front of the bank of monitors.

"See? On Monitor One we have the main entry area and the doorway to the B-4 Building Security Office." A flat, motionless electronic picture of the space he described appeared on the upper left monitor. "On Two we have the first floor corridor. On Three, the galley. On Four, the latrine. On Five, the main corridor in the basement. On Six—that's funny."

"What's funny?" Stevens demanded.

"We seem to have lost transmission from Camera Six in B-4. Probably just—"

"Freeze 'em!" Stevens ordered. "Stop erasing and stop recording on all B-4 cameras."

"Should I maintain transmission on the corridor cameras and freeze the rest?"

"I said all. Whatever's happened has already happened."

"Yessir."

"Where is Six supposed to be monitoring?"

"Um, lessee, Supply Room, basement."

"Jenkins," Stevens called over his shoulder to another guard, "buzz the duty officer in B-4 and tell him he has a problem in his basement Supply Room."

"Yessir," came from across the room.

"Play back what we have on tape from Six."

The young guard's fingers were already moving deftly over the keyboard. Indecipherable gray shapes flickered at high speed across the sixth monitor. The images on the other five monitors had frozen. Jagged, horizontal noise bars ripped across their screens.

The shapes on the sixth monitor stopped flickering and the screen shuddered into a normal picture. This picture consisted of Tony Martinelli's head, shoulders and upper chest, facing the camera, diagonally across the room from it. He was standing in front of a flat, white background. His expression conveyed at once swagger, boredom and indifference.

In an eyeblink this expression transformed. Surprise, incomprehension and feral terror replaced the arrogance. The new expression lasted for a heartbeat.

Then, a small, black mark appeared in the center of Martinelli's forehead. His head jerked backward. His body seemed to leap back. His head and shoulders then began to pitch forward. Suddenly, impenetrable, fuzzy, electronic snow replaced the image on the screen.

"Where's my father?" Wendy asked urgently.

"Hush," Michaelson told her, squeezing her shoulder decisively to emphasize the command.

But this admonition was unnecessary. Stevens was rattling out staccato orders and paying no attention to his two guests.

"Code 1," he barked. "Lockdown until further notice."

"Yessir," a voice behind them acknowledged amidst a sudden, raucous clamor of sirens and bells.

"Call the FBI Washington Field Office and tell them to get a scene-of-crime team out here as fast as they can."

"Yessir."

"Get six men with flak jackets and M-16s over to B-4 on the double."

"Yessir."

"I want a report from the duty officer in B-4 right now."

"Trying to raise him, sir."

"And call Internal Affairs at DOJ and tell them we have a situation here."

"Yessir."

Wendy turned around and looked at Michaelson.

"Will they let us stay here and find out what happened?" she asked.

"Unless I'm very much mistaken," Michaelson answered, "they will insist on it."

CHAPTER 10

Sweet Tony Martinelli lay face down on the floor of the B-4 Supply Room, diagonally across from the surveillance camera mounted in the corner nearest the door. The camera lens was shattered and the jack at the end of its transmission cord had been jerked out of the wall socket behind it. Martinelli lay in front of a neutral, cream-colored tarpaulin draped over something door-shaped that seemed a bit too small for a door.

On the floor in roughly the center of the room lay two small brass shell casings, a pair of white and blue cotton work gloves, and a long-barreled, semiautomatic pistol with a slanting, walnut grip.

"Colt .22 caliber Targetmaster," Smith said from the doorway, nodding toward the gun.

"What're the civilians doing here?" Stevens's deputy stage-whispered to his superior, nodding toward Wendy and Michaelson.

"That's exactly what I was trying to find out when things blew up," Stevens murmured in response. "He's got some reason for being here and until I figure out what it is, he's not going to be making himself comfortable in my office while I'm a quarter mile away, and he's not going to be wandering around the Administration Building asking people questions when I'm not there to hear the answers. As long as he's on the grounds, he's going to be wherever I am."

"Even a crime scene?' "

"Especially a crime scene. Now that this has happened, the only way I'm letting him out of my sight is when I see his taillights going through the main gate."

"You're the boss."

"Officer Smith," Stevens said then, "let's hear it."

"Yessir." Smith seemed to snap to attention, a throwback to his first career. "I was—"

"First things first, Smith. Are all of the other inmates accounted for?"

"Yessir. That is, well, I mean, sir, Martinelli's accounted for too, sir." Smith nodded toward the corpse. "I ordered a lockdown as soon as the trouble signal came, and all surviving inmates immediately complied."

"And has a search been undertaken of all inmate quarters?"

"In progress, sir."

"Very well, Smith. Now would you please tell me what you were doing when one of the inmates for whom you were immediately responsible was murdered, presumably by another of the inmates for whom you were immediately responsible?"

"Yessir. At approximately 12:50 P.M. this afternoon I had completed the morning's paperwork and I left the Building Security Office to make the rounds I usually make early in the afternoon work detail. As I was starting, inmate Banich came in the main entrance. The alarm went off when he went through the metal detector. It turned out he was carrying a rusty bolt from outside with the intention of throwing it away and he'd forgotten about it. I relieved him of that and had him pass through the metal detector again, to make sure he was clean."

"All right. Then what happened?"

"Approximately 12:57 P.M., continuing my rounds, I got to the top of the stairs at the back of the building. I heard someone coming up the stairs hurriedly—turned out to be inmate Gardner. Almost the same moment, I got the walkie talkie squawk from the Administration Building that there was a problem in the Supply Room."

"You're certain it was Gardner on the stairs?"

"Of course, sir."

"What did you do then?"

"I told him to return to his room. I hurried to the Supply Room in the basement and tried the door. It was locked. I unlocked the door, opened it, and found the scene you see here. I hit a button mounted on the wall a few feet from the door to activate the lockdown bell. I called for assistance and kept this room under surveillance until it came."

"All right. I take it there weren't any inmates in the Supply Room at the time you opened the door."

"You mean other than Martinelli, sir?"

Stevens glared at Smith.

"Ah, that is, sir, you are correct," Smith continued hastily. "There were no other inmates in the room at the time I opened the door, 12:58 or 12:59 P.M. at the latest, and there have been none in there since."

"And you have already told me that all of the inmates returned to their quarters in obedience to the lockdown bell, and have since been accounted for there."

"Yessir."

"Just let me be absolutely clear about this, Smith," Stevens said. "It is totally impossible for any inmate in B-4 to have left the Supply Room by any means from the time you got here and opened the door, at no later than 12:59 P.M., and the present."

"Yessir. For any inmate or anybody else."

His hands clasped behind his back, his face a mask of complacent dispassion, Michaelson carefully surveyed the Supply Room. He didn't see anything that looked very much like a false door or the entry to a hidden passage. Wooden shelves built from unpainted lumber took up most of the wall space. Paint, cleansers, toilet paper, paper towels, rags, scouring brushes, buckets and similar material filled up the shelves. Michaelson tried to imagine an adult slithering through the iron bars, spaced no more than three inches apart, on the window in the upper part of the opposite corner of the room. He concluded that that couldn't be done. Even if it could, he didn't see how the hypothetical slitherer could have gotten through the thick pane of glass that glared behind the bars and that appeared to be latched tightly shut from the outside. Stevens's questions seemed to Wendy to take on an ominous significance.

"Were there any visitors at B-4 today other than Mr. Michaelson and Ms. Gardner?" Stevens asked Smith.

"Nossir."

"Was any inmate assigned to any other building anywhere near B-4 any time today?"

"Nossir."

"Any guards, prior to the time you called for assistance?"

"Nossir."

"Any other authorized or unauthorized personnel of any kind?"

"Nossir."

"So the only people in or near Honor Cottage B-4 today, up until the time you found Martinelli's body and called for assistance, were the inmates assigned to this building, yourself, Ms. Gardner and Mr. Michaelson?"

"That is correct, sir."

"Did you see or hear any inmate other than Gardner anywhere in the vicinity of the Supply Room while you were making your rounds?"

"Nossir."

Stevens paused for a moment.

"Smith," he said then, "do you have any idea in the world how anyone could have gotten an unauthorized firearm into this Honor Cottage?"

"Nossir. Standard security procedures were in force at all times."

"What about the window?" Stevens demanded, nodding toward it. "I take it that glass can't be opened?"

"Negative, sir, it can be opened. The room has to be ventilated because we store paint in there. But it can only be opened from the outside."

"Smith," Stevens said, "if a bad person were outside, couldn't he open the window and throw a gun inside this room?"

"Well I suppose he could," Smith admitted, "but it'd set off an alarm—like Banich did with that bolt. The window's rigged with a metal detector, and all the metal detectors are tied into an alarm in the Building Security Office. The detectors on the windows aren't adjustable and they're not as sensitive as the one at the entrance, but anything the size of a gun would certainly set it off."

"How about part of a gun?"

"I beg your pardon, sir?"

"What if the gun were disassembled and thrown in a piece at a time?"

"I don't think so, sir," Smith said, shaking his head dubiously. "I'm sure that the clip or the barrel on that gun alone would be enough to trigger the window alarm."

Before Stevens could think of anything else to ask Smith, another subordinate announced the scene-of-crime team's arrival. A troop of men in blue overalls with FBI stamped in white block letters on the back bustled onto the scene. They bristled with cameras and compact, black, fitted attaché cases. The leader said his name was Clark Grissom and introduced the group perfunctorily to Stevens.

"Anything been touched inside?" one of them asked.

Stevens looked at Smith.

"Negative," Smith answered promptly. "Immediately after getting here and taking the steps I've already described, I walked far enough into the room to feel Martinelli's carotid artery with my fingertips and satisfy myself that he was dead, but otherwise there has been no entry and no exit since my arrival."

"Martinelli the decedent?" Grissom asked.

"Affirmative."

"Could anyone have been hiding in the room?"

"I don't see how. Look around if you like. You can see from here that there's no place for anyone to conceal himself."

"What's behind that tarp?"

"Not sure," Smith responded, a bit hesitantly. "Probably a mirror."

"What's a mirror doing down here?" Stevens demanded, incredulous.

"Awaiting repair, sir. Yesterday I directed inmate Stepanski to take the mirror from the Building Security Office down here so that it could be cleaned."

The FBI agents exchanged glances. Grissom looked at one of the other team members, who had been energetically snapping pictures and who nodded briskly.

Grissom walked over to the tarpaulin and pulled it away. This revealed the mirror that Smith had surmised was there. A substantial, cloudy blotch spread over the upper third of the glass.

"Okay," he said decisively. "We'll be at least forty-five minutes in here."

Michaelson, Wendy Gardner, Smith and Stevens responded to this hint by moving well away from the Supply Room doorway and walking toward the rear of the basement corridor.

"Have we got a rundown yet on what's on the frozen videotapes?" Stevens asked the subordinate who had told him about the scene-of-crime team's arrival.

"Yes. All cameras were frozen at 12:56 and 42 seconds. The entry area camera opens with the business between Banich and the metal detector that officer Smith described, after which they both move out of the range of that camera. This is followed by several minutes of an empty lobby."

"All right. Next camera."

"The ground floor corridor camera shows Banich policing the corridor and officer Smith walking down the corridor toward the back and eventually entering the stairwell, out of camera range. It was apparently frozen before inmate Gardner would have come into the picture."

"Clear enough. What else?"

"The galley camera shows nothing."

"That seems odd," Stevens said. "Smith, wasn't an inmate assigned to the galley this afternoon?"

"Yessir. Squires."

"Wouldn't he have shown up if he were there?"

"Yessir, unless for some reason he were standing directly beneath the camera."

"All right," Stevens said, nodding to the subordinate in civilian clothes, "go on."

"The latrine camera shows inmate Squires entering the shower room, removing something unidentifiable from his pocket, glancing around, and then retreating to a position that he apparently thought was hidden from the camera, but from which his left shoulder and arm were still visible."

"Okay. How about the basement corridor camera?"

"That one shows the following: inmate Lanier pushing a dustmop down the corridor, toward the stairwell; he stops near the Supply Room door, knocks on it, waits, knocks again, shrugs and starts pushing his mop again, this time in the opposite direction, toward the camera; then, when he's so near the camera that he's barely visible any more, inmate Gardner enters the picture from the right of the screen—that would be coming from the intersecting hallway and entering the corridor on the same side as the Supply Room door; Gardner walks to the Supply Room door, takes a key card out of his pocket, unlocks the door and goes inside; then, there's empty corridor again for a short time. . . ."

"How short?" Stevens demanded.

"Couple of seconds, maybe five at the most."

"Then what?"

"Then the door opens and Gardner comes back into the corridor in a hurry. He runs toward the back of the building and disappears into the stairwell.

"And we've still been able to raise nothing other than noise and what we've already seen from the Supply Room tape?"

"Right."

"What about the other two inmates? Where were they during this period?"

"Inmate Stepanski was working outside the building," Smith explained, "spraying the grass. McCutcheon was cleaning the first floor lounge."

"Okay. Has the search of the inmates' rooms turned up anything?"

"This," the subordinate said, showing Stevens a piece of sharpened tile. "We found that in Squires's room. Along with a quarter gram of cocaine. In Lanier's room we found fifteen-hundred dollars in cash, which is fourteen-hundred-and-seventy-five dollars over the maximum inmates are allowed to have by the regulations, but we didn't find anything else out of the ordinary."

"What about Martinelli's room?"

"Just this."

The subordinate put before Stevens a Polaroid photograph. It depicted a young woman with shoulder-length blond hair and a deeply tanned face, looking with cool appraisal directly at the lens. She was wearing a scarlet riding coat with black velvet facing on the lapels, ivory-colored riding pants, black, knee-high boots, and black gauntlets. In the white margin below the picture was written in neat, black, felt-tip pen, 3096.

"Hm," Stevens said.

"My reaction precisely," Michaelson commented. "May Ms. Gardner and I speak with her father?"

"You may not."

"I see. Do you think you'll be requiring us much longer?"

"Yes," Stevens said. His voice was a trifle chilly. "I think we will."

They did. The FBI spent another ninety minutes going over the Supply Room. After they had done that, they took statements from everybody, Michaelson and Wendy Gardner last. It was close to 4:00 P.M. before Grissom told Michaelson that he and Wendy could go.

"Thank you," Michaelson said as he stood up from the desk in the Building Security Office that Grissom had appropriated. "By the way. Do you have any explanation as to why no fingerprints were found on the apparent murder weapon?"

The thick-set, blue-eyed man looked up quickly.

"Your question assumes that no prints were found. I haven't said that that was the case."

"No, you haven't," Michaelson agreed. "On the other hand, you haven't asked to take my fingerprints or Ms. Gardner's, as you certainly would have done had you found anything on the gun."

"I'm not saying we did and I'm not saying we didn't," Grissom said. "But if we didn't, I'd guess it's because whoever did the shooting was wearing gloves at the time."

"Thank you again," Michaelson said. "Most illuminating."

"I wish we'd looked around the cottage more when we had the chance," Wendy said, dully and without real conviction, mostly to break the stiff silence she and Michaelson had ridden in for the first twenty minutes after leaving Fritchieburg.

"I don't think the FBI will miss much that we would have seen," Michaelson answered, then shook his head in irritation at his own peevishness.

Michaelson wondered why he hadn't told Wendy the first time she asked how his finger had been maimed. Bad form. No better answer than that. Just wasn't done. In the Foreign Service, everyone knew about that kind of thing and no one talked about it.

"This won't do," Michaelson said, mostly to himself.

He exited from the highway immediately after a white-on-blue sign that promised Food, accompanied by a drawing of a knife and fork for the benefit of any drivers whose verbal skills were unequal to that syllable. Wendy looked at him in surprise. Pulling into the drive-through lane of a McDonalds, he stopped at the window, ordered two black coffees and handed them to Wendy. Instead of heading back for the highway, he circled to the rear of the parking lot and backed the car into a space.

"We can talk freely here," Michaelson said.

"About what?"

"Anything at all. You can cry here, for example, if you feel like it. It won't bother me. If it would embarrass you to weep in front of me, you should feel free to go to the ladies' room and get your crying done there. But if you are going to cry, or remonstrate with me, or curse in frustration, or bemoan the situation on general principles, or do anything else essentially unproductive, please get it over with so that we can start to work. We have a lot to do and not much time to do it in."

Wendy stared at him in silence for a few moments. Steam from her coffee curled up in front of her face.

"I'm not going to cry," she said then.

"So much the better. Now then—"

"What are you so cranky about all of a sudden?"

"I hope I'm not cranky. I am a bit impatient. There's a difference, you know."

Another quiet moment passed while Wendy digested the

surmise that Michaelson was through talking to her like an indulgent uncle addressing a spoiled but adorable niece. That was what she got, she supposed, for telling him to stop patronizing her.

"You're right," she said after the three-second silence. "I'm sorry. I should be as impatient as you are. I know perfectly well that my father is incapable of killing someone—but everyone back there at that prison is absolutely certain that he murdered Tony Martinelli."

Michaelson's face softened. He took a sip of his coffee.

"Back at the prison," he said, "you told me that you wanted me to be completely honest with you, give you the whole story on everything I told you. Did you really mean that, or was that just for the record? Think before you answer."

"I meant it," Wendy said without taking an instant to think about the question. "I meant it exactly the way I said it."

"Very well then. In that case, I'll tell you that in my judgment what you just said is wrong on both counts."

"What do you mean?"

"First, I know Senator Gardner in many ways much better than you do. You know him as your father. I know him as a creature of Washington. I assure you that he is perfectly capable of killing a human being—and of doing so in cold blood and without a flicker of remorse."

"All right," Wendy said, keeping her voice low in an effort to control it. After all, she'd asked for it.

"Second," Michaelson continued, "while the gentlemen back at the prison no doubt suspect your father very strongly, it's clear that they are far from certain about his guilt."

"How can you be so sure?"

"Because if they were certain that your father killed Sweet Tony Martinelli, he would have left the Honor Cottage in handcuffs—and you and I might well have left it the same way."

CHAPTER 11

"Have you ever read *The Inspector General* by Gogol?" Michaelson asked.

"I doubt it. Is it in Cliff's Notes?"

"I'm not entirely sure. There was a movie made of it many years ago, though. Starring Danny Kaye, I believe."

"I must've missed it."

"Pity," Michaelson murmured.

He reached up to the dashboard of his Omni, where a plain cheeseburger and a plain hamburger rested on the paper sack he had flattened there. He and Wendy had finished their coffee before they had finished talking about what Michaelson wanted to cover, so Michaelson had made an excursion on foot back to the McDonalds whose parking lot they were using. He took the top half of the plain hamburger bun off and replaced it with the entirety of the plain cheeseburger.

"Why did you order something that had to be specially grilled?" she asked. "Doesn't that defeat the purpose of going to a fast food place?"

"At a place like this I always order something that I know hasn't been prepared in advance, so that I can be sure they'll have to put it together and cook it on the spot. It comes out hot and marginally less homogenous than the standard-issue stuff."

"Oh," Wendy said. "Why did you ask me if I'd read *The Inspector General*?"

"I think it explains why F. Whitmore Stevens was so accommodating to us back at the prison earlier today."

"How about if you explain it to me then?" Wendy proposed.

"Fair enough. In *The Inspector General*, the corrupt officials in a nineteenth century provincial Russian village get word that the Czar's inspector general is making his rounds, investigating abuses and hanging and flogging corrupt officials. They realize that when he hits their village they'll have to do everything they can to convince him that things are shipshape. About this time, a vagabond wanders into town. The officials believe that he's the inspector general in disguise. They proceed to fall all over themselves treating him like a prince."

"I don't understand yet."

"You and I, in perfect good faith, went to Fritchieburg as ordinary citizens interested in visiting an inmate we knew. Warden Stevens, however, apparently concluded that this was a clever disguise, and that we were secretly there in another capacity."

"Why do you say that?" Wendy demanded.

"Because he took more than an hour out of his busy day to escort us around his domain and otherwise shower attention on us. He could have had only two possible purposes for doing this. One: to impress us. Two: to figure out what we were up to."

"I give up. What were we up to?"

"Nothing. But the more we assured people we weren't up to anything other than visiting your father purely as private citizens, the more persuaded he was that we must have been playing a deeper game."

"Like what?"

"Like spying on the Department of Justice."

"Spying for who?" asked Wendy, for whom the objective case was as much a mystery as the masterpieces of Russian literature.

85

"The Department of State. Or, conceivably, the White House."

"But why would our government spy on itself?"

"To find things out."

"Well, obviously," Wendy sputtered. "But why—"

"Why create a cover story for a confidential emissary instead of just having someone on the President's staff or the Secretary of State's pick up the phone, call the Attorney General, and ask him whatever his or her boss wants to know?"

"Yeah."

"Because what they want to find out is something they can't reasonably expect to learn in that way. If the Secretary of State's staff makes that phone call, the response will be the bureaucratic equivalent of Go to Hell. If the President's staff makes it, the response will be evasion, delay and obfuscation."

"Why?" Wendy insisted.

"Ms. Gardner, you have just put your finger right on it. Why indeed?"

"I don't know."

"Nor do I. But there are possible reasons we could speculate about."

"Like what?"

"One: The information relates to an investigation that the Justice Department is afraid might be squelched for political reasons if word of it leaks out before enough evidence is assembled—an investigation of powerful congressmen in the same party as the administration, for example. Two: Someone is acting beyond his authority and wants to cover his tracks until it's too late to do anything about it. Three: Something embarassing has happened—something that you wouldn't want to see above the fold on the front page of the *Washington Post*. Four: Someone has made a deal that he suspects might not stand up very well to public scrutiny."

"Wow."

"A palindromic reaction not entirely inappropriate under the circumstances."

"You're making fun of me," Wendy said, her eyes suddenly blazing.

"You're right. I am and I shouldn't be. I apologize."

"Okay," she said then, instantly mollified. "But even assuming that there's something like that that someone in the Justice Department is worried about, why would Stevens think that we were the ones looking into it, rather than any other people who visit out there?"

"Good question. I know of no obvious answer. We have two clues. One: We came out to see your father. Two: My background is with the State Department and I'm reputed to have contacts in the offices of the executive branch that deal with foreign affairs and national security."

Wendy shook her head. Half of her Big Mac lay untouched and stone cold on a napkin unfolded over her lap.

"This is getting heavy," she averred.

"In more ways than one. All the more reason to get to work."

"Fine." Wendy's face snapped around and looked directly at Michaelson. "Where do we start?"

"We start by driving back to Washington and getting a good night's sleep. First thing tomorrow morning I have an appointment to see some gentlemen at the Department of Justice. I've begun to look forward to the meeting."

"What do I do?"

"You work on the number 3096."

"Where did 3096 come from?"

"That was the number printed on the bottom margin of the picture of that equestrian yuppie in Martinelli's room."

"Okay," Wendy nodded. "What do I do with it?"

"I'm not sure. I suppose it could be a dozen different things: a code, the last four digits of a phone number, the numerical part of a street address, a price, some kind of oblique time-and-date reference or something else."

"If it's a code, can we break it?"

"Not with only four characters." Michaelson looked through

the windshield while he chewed mechanically for a few moments. "We have to start somewhere," he said then. "Let's assume it's a phone number."

"Why assume that?"

"It's the most plausible of the possibilities I've thought of so far. No better reason."

"Why would someone write down just the last four digits of a phone number?"

"Because he was confident he could remember the first three but not all seven, and because he didn't want it to be instantly recognizable as a phone number if someone else saw it."

"Okay." Wendy looked dubious. "What do I do?"

"Get yourself ten dollars worth of quarters. Find a public phone. Start dialing that number, preceded by every three-digit prefix used in Washington and the surrounding area. When you get an answer, say that your're trying to find Tony and make a careful record of what the person you're talking to says."

"Is that all?" Wendy asked sarcastically.

"No. After you've done that, go to the main branch of the public library and ask to see the City Directory."

"What's the City Directory?"

"It's sort of a reverse phone book. Find an address for every phone number in this area that ends in 3096."

"All right." Wendy released a little explosion of breath. "Anything else?"

"A couple of things. One: While you're doing this, don't under any circumstances give your name, or address, or a phone number where you can be reached. Two: Don't try to contact me, especially at Brookings. Go to Cavalier Books on Massachusetts Avenue. I'll try to check in there at noon and four."

Wendy waited for a moment to see whether Michaelson would go on. The abrupt transition from schoolgirl-being-patted-on-the-head to subordinate getting precise instructions that were supposed to be unquestioningly obeyed had taken her a bit by surprise.

"Are you serious?" she asked, locking her blue eyes on his dark ones.

"Perfectly, Ms. Gardner," Michaelson said.

CHAPTER 12

"Mr. Michaelson, the United States Department of Justice takes an extremely dim view of people being murdered while in federal custody."

"An attitude shared by citizens and taxpayers," Michaelson assured the round-faced, flat-nosed man behind the desk. "At least by this one."

"If there's anything you'd feel comfortable telling me that might shed some light on the apparent murder at Honor Cottage B-4 that coincided with your presence at Fritchieburg, you'll find me most attentive."

"*Apparent* murder?" Michaelson asked softly, raising his eyebrows. "Surely you've ruled out the possibility that Mr. Martinelli died of natural causes?"

"Lawyerly reflex," the man said, shrugging. The other two men in the room smiled tolerantly.

The man behind the desk was about Michaelson's age. His salt-and-pepper hair was thinning. His brown eyes still glinted with the pugnacious *joie de guerre* of a career trial lawyer, even though it had been twenty years since he'd last addressed a jury. He was the Assistant Attorney General in charge of the Criminal Division at the Justice Department. His name was Frank Halloran.

Michaelson was sitting in a maroon leather mate's chair

in front of Halloran's desk. A yard or so away from Michaelson in a matching mate's chair sat an intense, thin-faced, brown-haired man in his early forties named Martin Billikin. He was in charge of the office responsible for prosecuting white collar crime—"crime in the suites," as it had come to be called. He was scowling.

Michaelson's appointment this morning had been with Billikin. When he had presented himself at the Justice Department, however, he had discovered that the conference had been expanded to include Halloran. Some wag once said that the Justice Department's White Collar Crime Office exists so that the graduates of Notre Dame Law School can keep an eye on the graduates of Harvard Law School. Billikin's manner suggested that he took that bromide rather seriously.

The last man in the room was in his mid-twenties. Halloran's introduction of the man had been perfunctory, and only five minutes later Michaelson no longer remembered his name. He sat on a nondescript couch against the inside wall of the office. He was writing furiously on a legal pad resting on his lap. He was the only one in the room taking notes.

This younger fellow's job, Michaelson surmised, was to prepare a Memorandum of Conference—memcon in the jargon. When the meeting was over he'd go back to his desk and draft what would amount to minutes of the session. Halloran and Billikin would review and revise the draft and when a version they were happy with had emerged that version would go into a file somewhere. Or, more likely, several files.

Why a memcon? Michaelson wondered. Why not a tape-recording or a stenographic transcript? Because those would be verbatim, he concluded. The memcon wouldn't. The memcon's version of the opening exchange between Halloran and Michaelson, for example, would read something like, "Mr. Halloran commented on the gravity of the situation represented by an inmate's violent death in federal custody. Mr. Michaelson said that he recognized this."

"One thing I can certainly tell you," Michaelson said to

Halloran, "is what I made this appointment to talk with Mr. Billikin about in the first place, before yesterday's unfortunate events."

"And that is what?" Halloran asked.

"The United States Attorney from former Senator Gardner's home state sent someone out to see Gardner not long ago. This person intimated that unless Gardner agreed to provide information about an unspecified and rather vague matter perhaps involving corrupt congressional dealings on a sugar-quota bill—although even that much is inference—the U.S. Attorney's office would oppose Gardner's soon-to-be-pending application for parole."

Halloran glanced at Billikin. Billikin said nothing, and the slight twitch in his facial muscles was indecipherable to Michaelson.

"No approach of that kind has been authorized by Washington," Halloran said. By Washington Halloran meant himself. "If some local U.S. Attorney is trying to manufacture a criminal investigation in an area as sensitive as that, he will either show us that he has something very tangible to go on or he'll get sat on."

"*If*?" Michaelson asked. "You mean he could be doing something like that without your knowing about it?"

Halloran nodded, without bothering to shrug.

"U.S. Attorneys aren't part of the professional civil service. They're political appointees, named by the President on the advice and consent of the Senate. They range from political hacks with delusions of grandeur to the cream of the local trial bar, serving out of a sense of civic duty. To a large extent, unless they screw up, they can run their own shops."

"I suppose one of them in the political hack category might believe that breaking a messy congressional scandal wouldn't hurt him in a later race for elective office."

"It's been done," Halloran conceded. "It's not the easiest way to get a political career started, but for a lot of guys it could be the only way."

"You know," Michaelson said then, "I can't help thinking that it's a bit too much to believe that the overture by the U.S. Attorney that Gardner described was a complete shot in the dark. It seems to me that he must have had some reason to hope that his approach would bear fruit."

"Is that a question?" Halloran said, smiling.

"No, I guess it isn't. But if there's something you'd feel comfortable telling me that might shed some light on the apparent anomaly, you'll find me most attentive."

"That sounds vaguely familiar."

"Why not? After all, it worked for you," Michaelson observed.

"That remains to be seen. I'll say this much: Anyone in Washington who says that the office he or she runs is leak-proof is either a liar or a fool. But the Criminal Division of the Justice Department is a lot closer to watertight than most of the outfits in this town. If anyone here told some cracker-barrel crimebuster out in the boonies about an investigation implicating congressional corruption, he'd find his ass over at the Environmental Protection Agency litigating toxic waste dumps in North Dakota in January so goddamn fast he wouldn't know what hit him." (In the memcon, this would come out, "Mr. Halloran said that unauthorized disclosure of information concerning the fact or substance of possible investigations involving other branches of the government would be viewed as a matter of the gravest concern.")

"I see. So, obviously, if your boldest subordinates wouldn't tell something like that to a Presidentially appointed United States Attorney, you're certainly not going to tell it to me."

"That is correct."

"There is one other thing I can tell you," Michaelson said. "I was reluctant to do so at first. When you hear what it is, you'll appreciate my reticence."

"I can hardly wait."

"I've decided to mention it because, after thinking the events of yesterday over carefully, it has become quite clear to me that former Senator Gardner is certainly not the one who killed Mr. Martinelli. Fortified by that certainty, I will advise you that Gardner regarded Mr. Martinelli's assignment to Fritchieburg in general and Honor Cottage B-4 in particular as extremely odd, and felt that Mr. Martinelli represented a threat to Gardner's own safety."

"What was his theory?" Halloran asked, his expression suggesting only the mildest interest.

"I don't know that he had worked out the details with any degree of rigor. I suppose one sinister interpretation would be that Martinelli might be there to frighten him so badly that he'd run to the authorities and beg them—that is to say, you—to listen to everything he knew about corrupt bargains in Congress."

"Do you believe that?"

"As a matter of fact I don't."

"Good. Because it isn't true."

"At the same time," Michaelson added, "I must say that Martinelli did seem to me to be stunningly out of place at Honor Cottage B-4."

Halloran paused for a moment before he responded. The youngest lawyer's blue Bic pen scribbled over the top page on his legal pad, clearly audible in the otherwise quiet room. Then Halloran spoke in a blunt, emphatic voice.

"Anthony Martinelli was assigned to the minimum security facility at Fritchieburg, and once there was assigned to Honor Cottage B-4, in accordance with sound policy properly applied. You have to understand, Mr. Michaelson, that since you are here in a non-official capacity there are certain things that I simply can't tell you."

"I have been made to understand that quite clearly."

"Anything that's a matter of public record, of course, is a different story."

You're getting old, Michaelson, the former FSO told himself. The man shouldn't have to draw you a picture.

"Public record," he said out loud, "The file relating to

the late Mr. Martinelli's latest scrape with the law falls in that category, I take it?"

"The portion of it filed in court certainly does." Halloran nodded at Billikin. Expressionlessly, Billikin produced from his briefcase a thin, legal-sized file in a brown, top-hinged cover. On the face of the cover was a typed label reading, *United States of America* v. *Anthony Martinelli,* Case No. 90-Cr-2402, United States District Court, Southern District of Florida.

Michaelson opened the cover. The material in the file was in reverse chronological order. Each item had a numbered tab on the margin. A typed table of contents was on top.

Michaelson glanced at the table of contents. The indictment showed up at tab 7. Michaelson knew nothing about criminal procedure, and was therefore puzzled. He looked more closely at the table of contents. Tabs 1 through 6 appeared to be identified as grand jury subpoenas *duces tecum,* addressed to different people. Beware of lawyers speaking Latin, he thought despairingly. No, wait. Buried in the middle of the subpoenas, tab 4, was something else. At least it didn't say subpoena. It said IDR.

Michaelson turned to tab 4. Printed in boldface across the top of the page was INTERDEPARTMENTAL DOCUMENT RE- QUEST. This particular IDR was one page long. It had gone from the Department of Justice to the Department of State. Michaelson spent forty-five seconds reading its text. It seemed like a very long forty-five seconds.

He closed the cover and handed the file back to Billikin.

"Is there any way that I could have a copy made of that file?" he asked Halloran. "At my expense, of course."

"Certainly there is," Halloran said. "Just file a request with the Freedom of Information Act officer on the first floor. We're usually able to respond within three weeks."

Michaelson smiled and stood up.

"Thank you very much for your time," he said.

* * *

Twelve minutes later Michaelson was wondering rather petulantly whatever had happened to soda fountains in drug stores. That used to be what a drugstore *was*: a place with a soda fountain that incidentally sold aspirin and several other things. Yet, on ducking into the first Peoples Drugstore he had come upon after leaving the Justice Department building, he had found no counter or tables to sit at while writing and, worse, no napkins to write on.

So he made do. He snatched a paperback at random from the bookrack, walked determinedly to the first available horizontal surface—it happened to be the camera and electronics counter—and began writing on the inside of the paperback's back cover. When he was through, some fifteen minutes later, he had reproduced the substance of the six categories of documents listed on the IDR he had seen for forty-five seconds in Halloran's office:

(1) Manifest of the ocean-going merchant vessel *Cracow*, MV [several digits], for a voyage taking place between February 10th and May 17th two years before;

(2) Demurrage certificates for the same vessel over the same time-period;

(3) International uniform straight bill of lading issued by Tracomex Corporacion, Tampico, Mexico on or about May 1st two years before covering a shipment to New Orleans, Louisiana, USA;

(4) Warehouse receipt no. T/M [several digits] brokered by Coudert Freres, New York City, during the period from April 25th to April 30th two years before;

(5) Letter of Credit No. [several digits] in the amount of $18,203,500 (U.S.), issued by the Mexican

National Bank, Mexico City, for the account of Planters & Traders Parish Brokerage, New Orleans, payable upon presentation of specified documentation to GUMCO; and

(6) A photograph of the *Cracow* riding at anchor at Tampico Roads, off the coast of Mexico.

When Michaelson had finished writing, he relaxed and straightened up. He noticed that a security guard and two cashiers were eyeing him rather warily, as if they expected him at any moment to begin declaiming about the wages of sin or the Fourth International. Michaelson was neither offended nor, upon reflection, surprised by this. It *did* look a bit peculiar, he supposed, to see someone go into a public place and spend a quarter of an hour beavering away at something in the back of a paperback book as if he were struggling with a piece of Talmudic exegesis.

Squaring his shoulders, he walked with immense dignity to the nearer cash register. Solemnly, he presented the book to the cashier and tendered $3.47 in payment for it. The cashier completed the transaction, looking Michaelson up and down uncertainly as she did so. She slipped the book into a sack and gave it to him. He imagined that he heard a collective sigh of relief when he finally walked out of the store.

CHAPTER 13

"Hello?"

"Uh . . . hi. Uh, could I please talk to Tony?"

"Who you wanna talk to?"

"Uh . . . Tony?"

"No one here nam' Tony."

"Oh. I must have the wrong number. Sorry to have bothered you."

"Thass awright."

Click.

Blip-blip-blip-3096. Ring . . . Ring . . . Ring . . . Ring—

"Hello."

"Uh . . . hi. Um, could I talk with Tony please?"

"I'm sorry?"

"Excuse me?"

"To whom do you wish to speak?"

"Uh, Tony."

"*Tony?*"

"Yeah."

"I'm sorry, but there is no Tony at this number."

"Oh."

"Good day."

Click.

Blip-blip-blip-3096. Ring . . . Ring—

"Silver Spring Laundry and Dry Cleaning. Debbie speaking, how may I be of service to you?"

"Uh . . . hi. I mean, could I talk with Tony?"

"Just a moment and I'll transfer you."

Ring . . . Ring . . . Ring—

"Tony Hansen here."

"Um, I was trying to reach Tony Martinelli."

"Who?"

"Tony Martinelli."

"Never heard of him. Anything I can help you with?"

"Uh . . . no, thank you."

Click.

1-blip-blip-blip-3096. Ring . . . Ring . . . Ring . . . Ring . . . Ring . . . Ring . . . Ring . . . Ring . . . Ring . . . Ring.

Click.

1-blip-blip-blip-3096. Ring . . . Ring . . . Ring—

"Yeah?"

"Uh, could I talk with Tony please?"

Click.

Wendy decided to review her notes before dialing the phone again. There are seventeen three-digit prefixes used with phone numbers in the District of Columbia. There are six used in northern Virginia. There are eight used in the part of Maryland surrounding D.C. This meant that there were thirty-one phone numbers altogether she had to check.

That seemed like an eminently manageable number. As the morning wore on, however, the chore Michaelson had assigned to her was getting to be a bit of a drag.

Thus far she had reached nine people who had told her that no Tony could be reached at the number she had dialed. She had established that someone named Tony, but not Tony Martinelli, did something at a place called Silver Spring Laundry and Dry Cleaning. She had come upon two numbers that were not in service. She had gotten no answer at four numbers, and no answer but a phone hung up in her ear at another. So she was a little over halfway through, except that she supposed she ought to make a couple of more tries at the no answers.

She sighed and went back to work.

It took her another forty minutes to complete the list. This is a long time to take to dial twelve telephone numbers, plus one more stab each at the numbers where there had been no answer the first time she had called. Considering that the average conversation, when any conversation occurred at all, lasted for no more than thirty seconds, it shouldn't have taken forty minutes to finish the assignment.

The truth was that strictly speaking Wendy didn't spend all of her time working at her task. There was a trip to the Coke machine. There was a visit to the ladies' room. There was a period of about seven minutes in a Designated Smoking Area out in the corridor. And then there were odd intervals spent staring into space, neatly redrawing the chart where she recorded the results of her calls, and otherwise procrastinating. And so it was with a feeling more of relief than of accomplishment that she finally finished.

She folded up her notepad, picked up her purse, and prepared to leave.

"Anything I can do to help?"

This question came from Randy Cox, whose office she was using and who chose this moment to saunter back into it. Wendy had disregarded Michaelson's instructions about using a public phone, preferring the desk and other amenities of a compliant acquaintance. She and Michaelson between them would make two critical mistakes this day, and this was the first one.

"I don't suppose you have a City Directory?" Wendy asked hopefully in response to Cox's question.

"No can do," Cox said. "That's one thing we don't have here. Anything else?"

"I guess not. Thanks a lot for letting me use your office. It was a major help."

"Don't worry about that. I saw the paper this morning. Anything I can do to help the senator I'm happy to do."

"Thanks, Randy. I really mean it."

"Okay. No problem."

Wendy smiled at Cox, then circled around his desk toward the door. Cox moved farther into the office to give her room.

"Look, Wendy," he said as she was about to go out, "do you mind if I ask you something?"

"Sure," she said, responding impressionistically to the general thrust of what Cox had said rather than to the actual words he had spoken. "Go ahead."

"What does the senator say happened yesterday?"

"I—that is, we, I mean I haven't had a chance to talk to him since the killing. The inmates were isolated before we were brought back to the B-4 building, and visiting hours were over anyway."

"So you don't really have any way of knowing what statements any of the inmates have given to the FBI?"

"No."

"I guess then you're basically just going on what Michaelson says he thinks the situation is?"

"Well, I suppose so, yeah."

"Wendy, can I make one suggestion?"

"Sure."

"Why don't you just call the senator and see what he has to say?"

"Randy, what are you trying to tell me?"

"The same thing I told you before. Based on everything I know and what everyone I've talked to says, Michaelson's worried about Michaelson. He's not worried about Desmond Gardner. If he thinks he can help himself by helping the senator he'll do that. But if he thinks he can help himself by burying your dad, he'll do that just as fast. If you think you can trust him, that's your decision. It just seems to me that the senator ought to be calling some of the shots here."

Wendy dropped what she was carrying back on the desk and used Cox's phone to call Fritchieburg. Honor cottage inmates were permitted to receive personal phone calls between ten and noon, although she wasn't sure what impact a recent homicide in an honor cottage might have on this privilege. When she asked the prison switchboard for Desmond Gardner, a brisk, bureaucratic voice informed her that inmate Gardner wouldn't be accepting any calls except from his lawyer.

Her father's lawyer was Jeff Logan. A call to his number produced the information that he was in court this morning. Did she care to leave a message?

She didn't. There wasn't any message for her to leave. She wrote the number down for future reference on an envelope that she thoughtlessly appropriated from Cox's desk and tucked the envelope into a dogeared copy of a tabloid weekly newspaper that she likewise commandeered. She'd doodled some offhand notes on the newspaper during her phone conversations, and she supposed she shouldn't leave them lying around where anyone wandering casually into Cox's cubicle might notice them.

"Look," Cox said as she prepared again to leave. "Don't forget what I said, okay? Anything I can do."

"I'll remember, Randy," she said. "Thank you."

She made her way to the street and looked for a cab to take her to the Martin Luther King Jr. Library. It was close to 10:30 in the morning. The total fruit of her labors consisted of a chart showing the results of calls to thirty-one telephone numbers ending in 3096. Diligent effort between now and noon might add an address for each of those numbers. That was what she'd have to show for her first morning's effort at clearing her father of murder.

CHAPTER 14

Michaelson sat placidly at his desk at Brookings, studying the list of documents that the Department of Justice had asked for from the Department of State in aid of prosecuting the recently deceased Sweet Tony Martinelli. He did this with a commingled sense of controlled excitement and growing satisfaction—something like the feeling you get in the midst of working the Sunday *New York Times* crossword puzzle when you know you're just about to figure out the theme, the leitmotif, the central conceit that will tell you the punning, multiple-word, twenty-seven letter answers to all the clues in quotation marks.

It wasn't that the array of documents conveyed any unambiguous message. The accumulated paper described on the IDR had a broad array of possible meanings. To figure out which of those meanings was the relevant one he'd have to look at the documents themselves.

How could he manage to do that? That, Michaelson was confident, was what was about to come to him.

There was something about the list that was odd—anomalous in the same way that the assignment of a mob enforcer like Martinelli to an honor cottage in a minimum security prison had been anomalous. What was it?

Patiently he read again through the list: a manifest; demurrage certificates; a bill of lading; a warehouse receipt; a letter of credit; a picture of a ship. Except for the photograph, as absolutely undistinguished a collection of ordinary, run-of-the-mill commercial documents as you could imagine. They were utterly common in their very specificity. . . .

That was it. The list was specific, detailed, pinpointed, focussed. Not "all documents arising from or relating to the loading, unloading, carriage, transshipment, sale, lease or other commercial transfer of any and all cargo carried by the merchant vessel *Cracow*, including but not limited to any and all shipping documents, packing slips" and so on. Not, in other words, what lawyers would write if they were on their own. Instead, a small number of particular documents.

Michaelson turned to a clean page on his legal pad. He unlocked the bottom drawer on his desk and pulled out the State Department Personnel Directory—not the one available to the general public but the classified one, the one showing the professional history of each FSO, the one whose distribution is now restricted because the Russians used to use it to spot CIA agents hiding behind State Department titles. What he was looking for was simple: Everyone who had both been in a position to see the documents on the IDR and pay attention to them two years ago, and had been in Washington around the time the IDR was prepared.

By 11:15, he had narrowed his list to five people. He wrote down their names and, opposite each name, the position that person had held two years ago:

(1) Bruce Simmons, Commercial Attaché, U.S. Embassy, Mexico City

(2) Charles Blair, Legislative Liaison, Western Hemisphere Affairs

(3) Sharon Fleming, Assistant for Commercial Matters to the Counsel for Western Hemisphere Affairs in the Office of Legal Advisor

(4) David Lewis, Desk Officer for Mexico

(5) Cynthia Broder, U.S. Consul, Tampico, Mexico

He called Simmons first. Simmons was in a meeting. Michaelson left a message.

He called Blair second. Blair was on another line. Michaelson left a message.

He called Fleming third. Fleming couldn't come to the phone at the—no, wait a minute, Mr. Michaelson, Ms. Fleming says she can take the call.

"Richard, this is a distinct pleasure. What can I do for you?"

"Nice of you to say so, Sharon. Listen, for reasons that I won't bore you with unless you insist, I find myself trying to reconstruct the adventures of a merchant ship called the *Cracow* that was apparently disporting in the Caribbean about two years ago."

"In a strictly unofficial capacity, of course."

"Of course. I have no capacities at the moment other than unofficial ones."

"Right."

"Anyway, I was wondering if you and I could have a talk about this sometime in the next few days?"

"I don't see why not, Richard. Let's see. How does next Tuesday morning look to you?"

"I'm very flexible, being retired and having so much time on my hands and so forth. Is ten o'clock all right?"

"Fine with me. How's Marjorie?"

"She's fine as far as I know."

"As far as you know. I'll see you Tuesday at 10:00."

"Thank you, Sharon."

"My pleasure, Richard."

Michaelson wrote Tuesday/10 next to Fleming's name. He had begun to dial Lewis's number when Simmons called back.

105

"Good morning," Michaelson said as he punched the button that aborted his own call and put Simmons on.

"Returning your call," Simmons said. Simmons was all business. Being a commercial attaché tends to do that to people.

"Yes, thank you for doing so. The reason I called is that, bizarre as it may seem, I've acquired an interest in the peregrinations two years ago of the *Cracow*. That's a mer. . . ."

"I'm familiar with the *Cracow*. What can I tell you about it?"

"What would be most helpful," Michaelson said in a woolly, absent-minded professor kind of way, "would be if I could sit down with you for about twenty minutes and see if you could confirm my own findings."

"Fine. 7:30 Monday morning."

"I'll see you then."

Michaelson wrote Monday/7:30 next to Simmons's name. He dialed Lewis. Mr. Lewis was on another line. Michaelson left a message.

He dialed Broder's number. Ms. Broder was away from her desk. Michaelson left a message.

Michaelson looked at his watch. It was 11:29. He drummed his fingers impatiently on his desk. If you've left a message in the morning, it really isn't good form to try calling again until at least the afternoon. He got up to get some coffee.

The phone rang. It was Broder.

"Thank you for returning my call," Michaelson began. "I doubt that you remember me. I was just finishing up at Near East and South Asia around the time you were coming on, I believe."

"We never worked together, but I've certainly heard of you," Broder told him.

"I'm calling about the *Cracow*."

"The *Cracow*?"

"Yes," Michaelson said. "It's a merchant ship, presumably of Polish registry, though that surmise would bear verification. It was plying the Caribbean about two years ago. That's about all I know about it, and for reasons that are honorable but quite mundane I would like to refine and augment that data somewhat."

"Can you tell me what the honorable but mundane reasons are?"

"Certainly. I'm at Brookings now. One of the younger fellows here is thinking of a monograph on the cost effectiveness of economic subsidies by the Polish government of its merchant marine. I was foolish enough to mention that I might be of help on some of the detail work and I'm afraid he took me up on it."

"You did warn me that it was mundane, didn't you? I really don't know very much about it. I vaguely remember a ship of that name docking at Tampico—that's in Mexico . . ."

"Yes."

" . . .while I was consul there. Why does that stick in my mind? Anyway, I'm not sure there's much else I could. . . ."

"Ms. Broder, I would find it very helpful if we could sit down face to face and just go over some notes I've made, to see if there's anything I've gotten wrong that you could clear up for me."

"I don't see any problem with that, although I'm afraid you'll be wasting your time."

They settled on Tuesday at 11:00.

Shortly after Michaelson hung up, the PBX operator at Brookings rang him to say that a David Lewis had called while Michaelson was on the phone with Cynthia Broder. Michaelson returned Lewis's return of Michaelson's first call. Lewis was on another line. Michaelson's lip thinned slightly—one of the few physical manifestations of frustration that he allowed himself. Would Michaleson care to hold? Michaelson said that he would be happy to.

Seven minutes later, Lewis came on the line.

"Sorry to hold you up, Mr. Michaelson."

Mister? Michaelson wondered if the United States was really picking people that young to be desk officers for countries as important as Mexico.

"Call me Richard, please. Mr. Michaelson is what people call my father."

"What can I do for you?"

"Well, I've put in my time at State and I'm over here at Brookings now, trying to think of ways to make myself useful. I've developed an interest in a merchant ship called the *Cracow* and its Caribbean voyage of about two years ago. I was. . . ."

"That's not a Mexican ship, is it?"

"I don't know, to tell you the truth. The name certainly doesn't suggest it, and the Eastern European countries don't go in very much for flags of convenience, but you can never be sure."

"The reason I ask is that Mexico has sort of been my bailiwick for the last two tours of duty and that's really the only area where I have any kind of detailed knowledge."

"The *Cracow* did apparently put in at Tampico during the period I'm interested in."

"Tampico?"

"Yes."

"Oh. Well, of course, a lot of ships put in at Tampico."

"I should think they do. The particular ship in which I have an interest is the *Cracow*."

"Oh."

"It occurs to me that this topic is perhaps not best discussed over the phone. I wonder if we could meet sometime next week and see what if anything you could add to what I know or substract from what I wrongly think I know."

"I suppose we could. How does next Friday sound?"

"It sounds fine if that's the best time for you. Tuesday at nine would actually be better for me," Michaelson said.

"Well . . . Tuesday. That might be a problem. Better make it Friday."

"Friday it is. Thank you very much. I'll see you Friday at 9:00."

That, Michaelson thought as he hung up, should give you plenty of time to check with your boss and find out whether I'm cleared for any intelligence more specific than the fact that a lot of ships put in at Tampico. He noted the date and time of his Lewis appointment on his list.

He checked to see whether there were any more messages for him. There weren't.

He glanced at his watch, 11:54. He had promised Wendy that he'd try to meet her at Cavalier Books around noon. He decided that he was too old to worry about form. He called Charles Blair again.

The phone rang six times. The State Department cafeteria is uncommonly good, as government refectories go, and several steps above the eating establishments within walking distance of the State Department building. Hence, it is usually crowded. As a result, clerical employees who can get away with it tend to sneak off a few minutes early for lunch. It's good to know these things. Just before the seventh ring, Charles Blair answered his own phone.

"Charlie. Dick Michaelson. I gather that the Department has survived my retirement."

"As much as it survives anything—which is to say, in a rather qualified way."

Michaelson wondered if he would have ended up talking like that had he gone to Dartmouth.

"Charlie, there's something you can do for me."

"What's that, Dick?"

"I'm in the private sector now, or what passes for it in Washington, and I don't have a title or a credential that I can throw at people any more to impress them or intimidate them."

"So you have to rely on your friends."

"Precisely. I would like, if I may, to speak with you for a few minutes at your convenience about a ship called the

Cracow and its trading exploits in and around our southern coast about two years ago."

"You said the *Cracow* is a ship?"

"Yes."

"That's one of those big things that goes in the water, like the locals are always blowing up over in the Near East?"

"Please don't make fun of me just because I don't fill out FSO efficiency ratings any more," Michaelson said, his voice still jovial.

"Sorry. Couldn't help it. You're in the right church but you've stumbled into the wrong pew. I'm basically a State Department lobbyist. I talk to congressmen. I know about quorum calls and unanimous consent. Ask me a question about international trade or ships on the high seas and you might as well be asking me about particle physics."

"You're being far too modest," Michaelson insisted.

"I'm altogether in earnest. I got roped into a discussion about international commodities trading about two weeks ago, for reasons that I still don't fully understand. Someone said that such and such commodities were fungible. I thought he was talking about baseball."

"Now, Charlie. . . ."

"You know who you should talk to is Bruce Simmons. He really knows his stuff in that area. I'd just be wasting your time."

"Why don't you let me be the judge of that?" Michaelson asked, the amiability in his tone now a bit insistent.

"All right, I'll tell you what. For old time's sake, I'll consent to expose my ignorance to you."

"Thank you."

"But you're going to have to give me a chance to prepare."

"Prepare?"

"Just send me a one-page letter identifying the topic— you know, the name of the ship, what was the big deal about it—and saying when you'd like to meet. That'll give me a chance to learn enough that I won't feel like a complete idiot."

110

"If you insist."

"Humor me. Oh, and Dick?"

"Yes?"

"Send a copy of that letter to Milt Daniels, will you?"

"The Public Information Officer? If I want a State Department press release I'll look in Tom Wicker's column."

"Just a formality. New policy. I'll be happy to talk to you, I just don't want anyone to think I'm cutting corners."

"Heaven forbid. Very well. You'll have your letter Monday morning if I have to type it myself."

"Thank you," Charles Blair said. "Have a good lunch."

Michaelson hung up the phone and looked out his window at Massachusetts Avenue.

"I'll be damned," he said softly to himself.

CHAPTER 15

"I refuse to believe that you are seriously asking me to do this," Marjorie Randolph said to Michaelson.

"I know that it's unreasonable, but. . . ."

"No, it's not *unreasonable*. Asking me to get the President to drop by for coffee and doughnuts in the morning would be unreasonable. Asking me to persuade a specific person in Washington, D.C., to accept a dinner invitation on slightly over twenty-four hours notice is preposterous."

"I'm only asking you to try."

"That's asking quite a lot."

"Washington is full of people who can do the difficult," Michaelson said. "Only you can accomplish the impossible."

"Your charm is going to get you into serious trouble one day."

"It already has. More than once. Please tell me that you'll do it."

"I'll try. I'll put in a good effort and I'll fail and then I'll remind you of what I said."

"Thank you."

"Only for you."

"By the way: has Wendy Gardner come by yet?"

"Yes, as a matter of fact. She's been here for at least fifteen minutes. You'll find her over in Foreign Affairs."

"Thank you again."

Foreign Affairs at Cavalier Books consisted of two six-shelf sections of paperbacks with titles like *Love's Barbaric Passion,* featuring on their covers drawings of young women with recently torn dresses and of men who, though supposedly hailing from no later than the eighteenth century and frequently from much earlier, looked like they'd just come from a delt-toning session on the Nautilus.

Michaelson found Wendy Gardner perusing the covers of these books, as if she might actually be thinking not only of buying one but of selecting it on something other than a random basis.

"Good afternoon," Michaelson said to Wendy as he approached. "I think that I've had a productive morning."

"Hello," she responded with that rockbottom, minimum level of sullen civility that women use with men when they want to let them know that they're furious with them. "I wish I could say the same thing."

"I detect a note of displeasure."

"Well, after all, you're an experienced diplomat."

"Did the phone-number-and-address project turn out to be more of a problem than I'd caused you to expect?"

"No." Wendy handed Michaelson the chart she had made summarizing the results of her efforts. "Unless you call wasting all morning on busywork a problem."

Michaelson glanced over the chart. Most of the numbers were for residences. A handful were for businesses. Most of those Wendy had talked to had said that no one named Tony could be reached at the number she'd dialed. Two had connected her to Tonies who were alive and well and who professed mystification at the reference to Martinelli. Three had hung up without comment and two she had never reached.

"I see," he said. "You've concluded that I sent you on a fool's errand."

"Well tell me something," Wendy rejoined. "Do you see anything terribly enlightening on that list?"

"It doesn't leap out at me."

"You mean you're not going to pretend that you have some colleagues at the CIA who can run that information through a computer and come up with some kind of brilliant new lead for us?"

"My former colleagues are all at the State Department. The CIA is a different group of chaps altogether. Always sitting on their briefcases when they're having lunch and that sort of thing."

"We don't know a single thing now that we didn't know yesterday afternoon. Not from this chart anyway. We don't even know that 3096 is part of a phone number, and even if it is we don't have any way to be sure that it's a Washington-area number instead of Miami or Chicago or Detroit or anyplace else."

"Excuse me," Marjorie called to them from an aisle-and-a-half away. "Why don't you two see if you can argue a little more loudly? There are a couple of people in Chevy Chase who can't hear you."

"She's right," Michaelson said to Wendy. "We are abusing Marjorie's ample hospitality. Why don't we go for a walk?"

"Where?" Wendy demanded.

"Well, how about down to the mall between the Washington Monument and the Lincoln Memorial and back?"

This was more walking than Wendy had done at one time since she'd gotten her driver's license, but she couldn't bring herself to tell someone three times her age that it sounded like too much for her. She followed him out of Cavalier Books and began strolling down Connecticut Avenue with him.

"I'm not sure the information you've gathered is as useless as you believe," Michaelson said after they had crossed Massachusetts. "It would have been nice if someone at one of those numbers had said something suggestive of a connection with Tony Martinelli, but the fact that no one did may only mean that someone is being very careful—something you'd expect of a professional criminal."

114

"I'll be more than a little surprised if any hardened criminals turn up at Silver Spring Laundry and Dry Cleaning."

"I'll grant you that the addresses seem anodyne. But that's not conclusive either. A small business or a private residence can still be the scene of drug sales or numbers running or a variety of other criminal enterprises that could well have some bearing on Martinelli's death."

"How do you propose we find out about these particular addresses?"

"I can't say that I've given the matter a lot of thought. Perhaps we should put that question on hold while we review what I've been able to find out. Maybe an answer will suggest itself."

"Okay," Wendy said dubiously.

Michaelson described his conversation at the Justice Department. Wendy listened with manifest and growing impatience, and then offered him a you-mean-that's-it? expression when he was finished.

"In other words, they told you nothing."

"Next to nothing, that's correct."

"I thought you told me your morning was productive. You didn't learn a thing."

"On the contrary, I learned a great deal. You can learn things without having people tell them to you, you know."

"Like what?"

"Oh, for example: There's an investigation under way into something that your father might plausibly know something about, and that's why the U.S. Attorney back home made the approach that he did."

"Why do you say that?"

"Because the high mucky muck that I was talking to at Justice went out of his way to convince me that, although word of a criminal investigation could theoretically be leaked by his division, it probably hadn't happened in this case."

"How do you get from there to the conclusion you just handed me?"

"If there were no investigation, then there would have been nothing to leak and he could confidently have guaranteed me that no leak of any such matter had come from any of his people. Since he hedged his bet, there must have been some risk that such a leak had in fact occurred. Therefore, there must have been something that could have been leaked. Hence, there must be an investigation going on."

"Why would he care so much about your opinion that he'd go to that kind of trouble to cover his ass—er, fanny?"

"I doubt it was any trouble at all. I imagine it's second nature to him. But as to why he should care, the only answer I can think of is the inspector general hypothesis."

"Do you really think that theory makes any sense?" Wendy asked.

"I'd certainly have my doubts if it weren't for one thing."

"What's that?"

"I can't think of any other reason why he would have led me by the hand to the court record in Martinelli's case."

"Tell me why you think he did that, and why that means that you're the inspector general."

"All right. He did it because he wants to be sure he has it both ways. If I really have some secret but powerful mandate, then he comes across as being savvy and reasonably cooperative. If I don't and somebody who does looks into this whole thing later on, then the paper record will show that he revealed absolutely nothing to me beyond what I had a statutory right to see."

"Then why didn't he let you copy the file?"

"Because if I really were the inspector general, I'd be able to retrieve the entire contents of the file myself, very quickly, once I knew there was something in it worth looking for. If I turned out not to be the inspector general, then he wouldn't have appeared to have been unduly accommodating to me. Fortunately from our standpoint, unfortunately from his, I have a rather good memory."

"All right," Wendy said. She pronounced the words with

116

a long exhalation, as if she were exhausted by the effort of listening to Michaelson.

They had reached the front of Lafayette Park, directly across Pennsylvania Avenue from the White House. Beside the west wing, the old Executive Office Building with its improbable but majestic tiers of pillars and casements loomed in government-issue grayish-brown. Beside the east wing, a long line of tourists patiently waited for admission to their chief executive's residence, while Masterpiece Theatre voices on tape recordings told them over loudspeakers what they'd see on the inside.

Michaelson and Wendy crossed Pennsylvania and walked past the east side of America's most famous address. The Washington Monument loomed only a few hundred yards and one very busy street beyond them. They walked toward it.

"All right," Wendy said again after they had crossed Constitution and begun walking down the mall, "tell me what else you learned."

Michaelson told her about his five phone conversations with the people at State.

"So you think you might learn something when you talk to them next week?" she asked when he was finished.

"It's an outside possibility, I suppose. Actually, I think that I've already learned the thing I'd hoped to learn by making the calls."

"Namely—what?"

"That Charles Blair leaked some rather sensitive information to the Department of Justice."

"What makes you think it was Blair?"

"A very fair question. Call it oblique inference. He was the only one of the five people I talked to who tried to steer me to one of his colleagues. And he was the only one to insist that I generate a letter documenting our talk and our appointment."

Wendy stared at him.

"You don't seem convinced," he said. "I can't really say I blame you. It's the best I can do."

"It's all oblique inference," Wendy said, sighing. "It reminds me of Psych 10."

"Oh?"

"Yeah. Last term I took the introductory course in Psychology. The morning of the first class, one guy came in about five minutes late. The grad ass (this is what undergraduates call graduate assistants) who was teaching the class says, 'Five minutes late—obviously suffering from avoidance neurosis.' So the guy says that next class he'll come five minutes early. 'That would be anxiety neurosis,' the grad ass says. So then this other kid says, 'What about me? I was here exactly on time.' And the grad ass says, 'Obsessive-compulsive. You see, you all have a neurosis. It's just a question of which one.' "

"I'm not sure I altogether grasp the application of this anecdote to the problem before us."

"The point is, the grad ass had the rules set up so that there was no way for him to be wrong. No matter what you did, he could pin a neurosis on you."

"I see. And you're saying. . . ."

"I'm saying it's the same thing here. If somebody spills his guts to you, then that proves that he's telling you what he knows because he thinks you're the inspector general. On the other hand, if some guy practically totally stonewalls you and just gives you little hints to be polite, that proves that there's a lot of great information somewhere between the lines of what he said, and he dropped the hints because he's afraid you might be the inspector general. Finally, if a bunch of people tell me absolutely nothing, that proves that one of them might have something to hide. So according to you, no matter what results your suggested investigations produce, we must be on the right track."

"You're right."

"I was afraid of that."

"I believe it was Karl Popper who contended that no discipline could qualify as a science unless its hypotheses were subject to refutation by the results of empirical observation.

118

If whatever theory you have is set up in such a way that no matter what happens it's consistent with that theory, then it's not a scientific theory."

"I guess that's kind of what I was saying."

"Unfortunately, no one's come up with a scientific theory that satisfactorily deals with the winks and nudges and raised eyebrows that pass for communication in Washington. All I can tell you is, I've been at this for a long time. I've been right a lot more often than I've been wrong. My best judgment is that the conclusions I've drawn so far are correct."

"Have you considered the possibility that you've been at it too long?" Wendy demanded.

"Yes, that thought has crossed my mind once or twice."

"I mean, it seems to me that there's a possibility that, you know, we haven't even considered yet."

"And what possibility is that?"

"The possibility that dad does know something—something that could be very damaging to powerful people in the government."

"Or outside it," Michaelson nodded.

"And that Martinelli was assigned to Honor Cottage B-4 because his job was to shut my father up."

"By killing him, you mean."

"That's right."

"I have considered that theory, but I rejected it as too improbable to warrant diversion of any of the scarce investigative resources we have at our command. It's an interesting premise for the kind of people who write novels and aren't encumbered by any knowledge of the way government actually works, but it's not very high on the scale of real world possibilities."

"How do you know that?" she demanded.

"There is no one in the United States government, including the President, who can get an American citizen on American soil killed just by picking up the telephone and giving an order that it be done. The executive branch isn't a pyramidal monolith directed from the top down as business corporations supposedly are. It is a collection of competing interest groups coexisting in uneasy tension."

"So what?"

"So, the Gardner execution theory assumes that at least two elements of this collection—say, the White House staff and the Bureau of Prisons—collaborated in some way in an effort to murder an American citizen to keep him from telling something he knew."

"And that couldn't have happened?"

"Ms. Gardner, there is nothing that your father could possibly know that could conceivably be as damaging to anyone as the revelation of such a homicidal conspiracy would be. It wouldn't make any sense to kill Desmond Gardner in order to shut him up if by the very act of killing him you put infinitely more damaging information in the hands of several other people who could reveal it in the future."

As soon as he had finished his answer, Michaelson saw from the waves of dismay washing across Wendy's face that he'd made a mistake—that instead of convincing her that he was right he had only reduced whatever confidence she had in his judgment.

"Do you mind telling me," he asked her then by way of diversion, "whether anything in particular has happened today to raise this specific possibility in your own mind?"

"Well, one thing."

"To wit?"

"I tried to reach dad by phone. The prison said that he'd left instructions that no calls were to be put through to him except from his lawyer. And his lawyer is incommunicado."

"Does that alarm you?"

"It surprises me. Why shouldn't dad take a call from me, unless there's something he's afraid to tell me?"

"Because he's now a veteran of the American criminal justice system. One thing that he has had drilled into his skull is that in connection with any potential crime or criminal charge he must not under any circumstances tell the police anything, except on the advice of his lawyer."

"We're not talking about the police. We're talking about me."

"Not only you, unfortunately. Because your father is in prison, the government has the right to open every piece of mail he receives and listen in on every phone conversation he has. The only exception is for communications with his lawyer."

"But he didn't do anything," Wendy protested.

"All the more reason not to help anyone trying to prove that he did. More important, he has your involvement to consider. When you first talked to me, you told me that your father thought his life might be in danger. Somebody brought a firearm into Honor Cottage B-4, and that firearm was used yesterday to kill the man your father had identified as the source of his fears."

"You're not saying that I smuggled that gun in there?"

"Of course not. But put yourself in your father's position: If you were he, could you be absolutely sure?"

They had reached the Lincoln Memorial. They stood in the vibrant April sunshine between the reflecting pond and the marble monument, looking toward the path that led to the Vietnam Memorial.

Wendy was experiencing something entirely new to her, something for which nothing in her background or education had prepared her: doubt. For the first time, a mind that had always been secure in perfect if often erroneous certainty began to wonder—what if?

"Anything else we should talk about at the moment?" Michaelson asked.

"No," Wendy said slowly. "I don't think there is."

"I'll see you at Cavalier Books at 4:00."

121

CHAPTER 16

The lunch-hour rush at Cavalier Books lasted until 2:00 P.M. Marjorie Randolph waited until it was over before embarking on the impossible assignment she had accepted from Michaelson. Promptly, at 2:01, she walked determinedly back to the store's small stockroom, sat at her functional desk, and consulted a battered address book with a black, leatherette cover. She had to look through half a dozen names before she found the one she wanted.

She dialed a number and listened to the phone ring twice.

"Department of State," a gender-neutral voice answered.

"May I speak with Mr. Morton please?"

"Just a moment."

One more ring.

"Mr. Morton's office."

"Hello, Cynthia, this is Marjorie Randolph at Cavalier Books."

"Oh, hello," Cynthia Brooks said. "Did you want to speak to Mr. Morton?"

"No, actually, I wanted to speak with you. Do you have a moment?"

"Of course."

Of course. The State Department hadn't been pressed for time since early in the Kennedy administration.

"Well, I was calling to tell you that we have a new shipment of English mysteries, eight titles, that won't go on the shelf until Saturday at noon. One of them is a new John Wainwright, and there's a new Jennie Melville as well. I thought that you might want to come down for an early look at them."

"Marjorie, you living, breathing doll. I'll be there promptly at nine Saturday morning."

"Well, bring some coffee. We don't open until 9:30."

"Half-past, then. Thank you very much, Marjorie."

"Happy to be able to be of service. Can you transfer me to another number at State or do I have to dial in again?"

"I can transfer you. Whose number do you want?"

"Charles Blair's. His secretary is actually the one with whom I'd like to speak."

"Oh, does she like cozies too?"

"No, I only allow myself one specially favored customer per agency. I'm calling her for something entirely different. I'm supposed to try to get Mr. Blair to a dinner party, and I thought I'd have a better chance if I had some idea of what his schedule looks like. In fact, if you could smooth the way for me I'd very much appreciate it."

"It's the least I can do," Cynthia said. "Hang on."

There followed a delicate sound rather like an electronic sigh. Marjorie waited in telephonic limbo for several seconds and then heard Cynthia come back on the line.

"Marjorie, do I still have you?"

"Yes."

"And you're on, Gloria?"

"Yeess," a trilling voice said patiently.

"Very well," Cynthia said. "Gloria, Marjorie Randolph is a very great friend of mine. She's trying to arrange an invitation for your boss, and she needs to know when would be a good time."

"When were you thinking of generally?" Gloria asked.

"This week," Marjorie hedged, reluctant to come right out with something as absurd as tomorrow night.

123

"Oh, I don't think you have much hope of that," Gloria clucked. "Mr. and Mrs. Blair are having an affair this evening. McRobert Pond will be there and some media people, and Mr. Blair has told me a dozen times he expects it to be dreadfully boring. I'm afraid he and Mrs. Blair will be partied out for this week by the time that's over."

"There's no hope at all, you don't think?" Marjorie asked.

"Nope. None at all."

"Oh, well. Thank you for your help. See you Saturday, Cynthia."

The three women exchanged goodbyes and Marjorie hung up.

No hope at all, she thought to herself. This is going to be more of a challenge than I thought.

"Do you have an appointment to see Mr. Logan?" the young woman at the reception desk asked Michaelson.

"I do not. I'll be happy to wait. I'd appreciate it if you'd tell Mr. Logan that I'd be obliged for five minutes of his time at his convenience this afternoon to talk with him about his client Desmond Gardner."

"He's in conference right now. He could be tied up for some time yet."

"As I said, I'll be happy to wait."

Michaelson sat down and began to leaf through a copy of the *ABA Journal*. An article on an organization called Lawyers Without Frontiers, dedicated to bringing the benefits of American litigation technology to mass-tort victims in the third world, caught his eye. The receptionist, with what appeared to be infinite reluctance, called Jeff Logan's secretary to relay Michaelson's message.

"Marjorie, I really don't feel comfortable doing this."

"Good for you. I wouldn't have the nerve to ask you

except that it's the only way I can think of to accomplish something Richard specially asked me to accomplish."

"I understand how important that is to you and you know how much I want to help, but I don't even know the man."

"All you have to know about McRobert Pond is that he's the most libidinous Senior Fellow—that's capital *S*, capital *F*—at the Pierpont Endowment for the Republic," Marjorie told her young assistant manager as she maneuvered her into the stockroom.

"What's the Pierpont Endowment for the Republic?"

"It's a think tank with offices two floors above the Carnegie Endowment for International Peace. It's sort of a government in exile for the party that's out of power at the moment."

"What will I say to him?"

"Just say that he probably doesn't remember you but you met him at a reception a few weeks ago while you were a student intern at Carnegie, your name is Carrie, and you happen to be in Washington tonight and you wonder if he'd like to have a drink with you this evening."

"But none of that is true. Except my name."

"Of course it isn't, Carrie, love. It is true, however, that there are periodically student interns at Carnegie, that Pond occasionally meets them, and that the only thing he remembers about any of the female ones is how much he'd like to sleep with them, which is invariably a lot."

"But how. . . ."

"It is also true that on the telephone you sound like the kind of woman who inspires in men fantasies worthy of Henry Miller."

"But what. . . ."

"I guarantee you that Mr. Pond will pretend to remember you and will accept your invitation with alacrity. All you must remember is that you're only going to be in Washington tonight and that you must meet at seven o'clock—no earlier and no later."

"But what if I don't like him?"

125

"You certainly won't like him, precious goose. He's a snake."

"But I'll be—leading him on, won't I?"

"Not for long. Let him buy you a drink. Look into his eyes while he discourses at length on the International Monetary Fund. Nod occasionally."

"That's not leading him on?"

"Then, when he puts his hand on your knee and suggests that the two of you adjourn to someplace with a horizontal surface, throw the rest of your drink in his face, assert with outraged dignity that he has obviously misapprehended your intentions, stand up, stamp your pretty little foot, and walk out."

"I wouldn't do this for anyone but you," Carrie said.

Her face a portrait of misgiving, Carrie dialed the number Marjorie gave her for the Pierpont Endowment for the Republic. To her astonishment, she reached McRobert Pond without difficulty and the conversation ensued exactly as Marjorie had said it would.

Wendy Gardner was visibly moping when she walked back into Cavalier Books just before 3:00. With the ebbing of certainty had come dissipation of the intellectual energy that depended on it. Disspirited and psychologically adrift, she no longer knew what to think or whom to believe. The mental stamina necessary to reason critically through the information she had eluded her. Emotionally, she had reached a point analogous to the twelfth mile of a marathon for a half-trained runner; she didn't collapse; she just said the hell with it and dropped out of the race.

Wendy still had the copy of *D.C. After Dark,* the tabloid that she'd taken from Cox's office. Bringing it over to the tea-and-coffee bar, she paged listlessly through stories about upcoming rock concerts, record and film reviews, columns of iconoclastic opinion, and reams of personal ads.

* * *

"Hello. This is Jennifer Blair. I'm not able to come to the phone right now, but if you'll please leave your name, number and a brief message at the tone, I'll try to return your call."

Beep.

"Hello, Jennifer. This is Marjorie Randolph at Cavalier Books. I just wanted to let you know that the copy of *Ladies' Own Erotica* that you asked us to order for you is in. It'll be up by the cash register with your name on it whenever you find it convenient to drop by."

Marjorie hung up the phone. If that doesn't draw a call back in under sixty seconds, she said to herself, party tonight or not, I'll give Carrie a raise.

The phone rang less than half a minute later. Marjorie answered it.

"Cavalier Books," she said.

"Marjorie? This is Jennifer Blair."

"Oh, hello, Jennifer. I'm glad you got my message."

"Marjorie, there must be some mistake. I didn't ask you to order a copy of . . . that book for me."

"You didn't? My word, I wonder how that happened. Oh, well. No harm done. I'll just take your name off and put the book on the shelf. Thank you for calling, Jennifer."

"You're welcome."

Here we go, Marjorie thought. McRobert Pond was a jerk, and you certainly couldn't count on him to phone his hostess with an eleventh-hour decision to bail out of her party. Pond's secretary, on the other hand, was a peach, and Marjorie was certain that she would have seen to it that Jennifer Blair got the unwelcome but essential news immediately after Carrie's seductive phone call to Pond. Michaelson was an obvious substitute for Pond, and Jennifer Blair could hardly help thinking of Michaelson when she talked to Marjorie.

A pause of one second ensued. The agony of Jennifer

Blair's indecision seemed palpable to Marjorie over the line, and she wondered if her own suspense were equally apparent.

"Uh, Marjorie," Jennifer Blair said then, "as long as I have you on the line. . . ."

"Yes, Jennifer?"

"You know Richard Michaelson, don't you?"

"Yes, he comes in here occasionally. I'm expecting him later this afternoon, in fact."

"Do you know where I might reach him?"

"Well, he has an office at Brookings, but I happen to know he's away from there for the rest of the day." Marjorie counted silently to three. Then she dropped the other shoe. "You see, Richard and I are going out this evening."

"I see. Marjorie, I wonder if I might ask you a very great favor."

"Of course you may, Jennifer."

"The thing is, Charles and I are planning a small dinner tonight, and I've had a last-minute cancellation that's rather a bore. If you could spare Richard this one night, it would help out enormously."

Marjorie glared indignantly at the mouthpiece. Plebian, she thought.

"To fill in, you mean?" she said sweetly to Jennifer Blair.

"Yes. I know that it's ridiculously short notice, but. . . ."

"Well, Jennifer, Richard and I have nothing specific planned for tonight, but I couldn't break a date with him that I'd already agreed to. My sainted mother would come back from the grave to upbraid me mercilessly."

"Oh, Marjorie, you would *both* of course be more than welcome."

That's one thing I like about you, Jenny old girl, Marjorie thought. You know when you're licked.

"In that case," Marjorie said, "I think you can count on us."

"Thank you ever so much, Marjorie. Drinks from 6:15, dinner promptly at 7:00."

"Thank you for inviting us. We'll see you this evening."

Marjorie hung up. She walked back into the store proper, humming "The Four Seasons." She felt just short of giddy with satisfaction. Richard had been right. The task he'd set her had been impossible. She had nevertheless accomplished it, and she was probably the only person in Washington who could have done it.

Her high spirits lasted until her eyes fell on Wendy Gardner, looking like someone who had been jilted by her first love, failed the bar exam, and been told that Margaret Mitchell had plagiarized *Gone With the Wind* all in the same afternoon. Marjorie assumed that Wendy's crestfallen demeanor had something to do with the project Michaelson was working on with her, so she decided that she might as well get to the bottom of it.

Marjorie walked gingerly toward the small platform with its two tiny tables. When she reached Wendy's table, she waited for a moment to see if Wendy would glance up long enough from the personals in *D.C. After Dark* to notice her. Despairing quickly of that possibility, Marjorie decided to plunge ahead.

"I trust that you and Richard got things cleared up between you," she said.

Wendy glanced up, startled and a trifle confused.

"Oh, uh, yeah, I suppose so," she said.

Wendy remained seated and Marjorie remained standing. Wendy seemed dimly aware that there was something anomalous in this situation, but appeared to have no clue as to what to do about it.

"If you'll forgive my saying so," Marjorie continued, "you seem a bit out of sorts over the whole thing."

"I guess so," Wendy responded. "Uh, look, would you, uh, like to sit down or something?"

There may be hope for her yet, Marjorie thought as she dropped gratefully into the chair opposite Wendy.

"Thank you. He's very good at what he does, you know. Richard, I mean."

"I'm sure he is," Wendy said with a shrug. "But, uh, he's not really very nice, is he?"

"Nice?" Marjorie blurted, unable to suppress the smile that played around her lips.

"Yeah. Nice. What's so funny about that?"

"Well," Marjorie said judiciously, "it's a little bit like saying that a surgeon isn't clumsy or that an engineer isn't particularly poetic. I mean, *nice* isn't really what you look for in a Foreign Service Officer. Richard is loyal, competent, morally and physically courageous, charming when he wants to be, vastly interesting to talk to and be with. But I have to agree with you. He certainly isn't very nice."

"Then why do you like him so much?"

"Charming and vastly interesting are what appeal to me. That and the fact that he never kids himself."

"What's that supposed to mean?" Wendy persisted.

"Maybe we're just having trouble finding a common language here," Marjorie said. "Maybe I can give you an example. Richard and I had our last discussion about the war in Vietnam six months after Nixon's inauguration. I was morally certain that he no longer believed in the position he defended. I told him he was losing his son over the war. He said, 'A lot of Americans have lost their sons over this war. I took an oath to serve my country.' I almost hit him. I said, 'You can serve your country when it's right.' Do you know what he answered?"

Wendy shook her head.

"He said, 'My country doesn't need me when it's right. When a country's right, most any well meaning bachelor of arts will do.' "

Marjorie realized that this reminiscence had about as much resonance for Wendy as an airy allusion to Crecy and Agincourt would have. Before she could come up with anything more concrete, however, Carrie called over the information that Michaelson wanted her on the telephone.

"Excuse me a moment, if you would please," Marjorie

said, and threaded her way through the store to the nearest extension while Wendy returned her attention to the personals.

"Hello, Richard."

"Hello, Marjorie. I'm just on the verge of getting in to see Senator Gardner's lawyer, and I thought I'd call and see if you'd had any luck on the Blair project."

"Well, in a manner of speaking I have."

"By all means tell me about it."

"Under no circumstances would the Blairs accept an invitation from us for tomorrow night or the night after."

"Unfortunate."

"Fortunately, however, the Blairs themselves are having a dinner tonight."

"Splendid. And you think I might be able to crash the gate?"

"Actually, Richard, they have invited you—but only on the condition that you bring me along."

"*T'es formidable,* Marjorie. You are a marvel."

"If you're going to speak French, Richard, please do get the pronunciation right."

"My pronunciation is impeccable."

"Impeccably American. We should try to be there by 6:45."

"I'll pick you up by 6:30. Thank you immensely."

"Very good, Richard. You're quite welcome."

Marjorie hung up and turned back toward the table where she and Wendy had been sitting, with the idea of returning to continue her conversation with the young woman. But the table was empty and Wendy was gone.

CHAPTER 17

"When your most recent service to a client was to represent him at his sentencing," Jeff Logan said, "I suppose you can't be particularly surprised when he rejects your advice."

On this note of mordant self pity, Logan shifted his gaze so that he was looking over Michaelson's right shoulder at the view of Benjamin Franklin and the old Post Office Building visible through his office window.

"Your advice, I take it, related to me?" Michaelson probed.

"Yes. Once that dead body turned up in the vicinity, I told Desmond Gardner that he oughta drop you like a bad habit. 'No one from the government is there to help you, no one from the government is your friend.' That's what I told him."

"I take it he wasn't persuaded."

"You wouldn't be sitting here if he were. His instructions are for me to tell you whatever you want to know, since he can't safely do it himself. I don't like it, but it's his call."

"Well then, perhaps you could begin by telling me what Gardner's own account of his conduct around the time of the killing is."

"Pretty simple," Logan shrugged. "He was supposed to give the tile in the lateral basement hallway a once over. He lugged his bucket and stuff over there and slogged away for awhile. Then he decided that it was a pretty dirty job and he wanted the pair of work gloves that he wears when he cleans the latrine."

"The gloves weren't issued to him when he began that afternoon's work detail?"

"He says no. Anyway, he went out the basement door to look for Stepanski to get the card key to the Supply Room so he could get the gloves."

"Stepanski was working outside?" Michaelson asked.

"Yes. Stepanski assigned the jobs, and according to Gardner he always gave himself something outside if he could."

"Very well. Sorry to interrupt. Please go on."

"Okay. Gardner found Stepanski in back of the building, spritzing the grass with fertilizer or something. He talks him out of the Supply Room card key and goes back in the building through the basement door."

"Wait a minute," Michaelson said. "I thought that the basement door could only be opened from the inside, except by guards."

"That's right," Logan conceded. "Gardner was heading around to the front of the building to go in by the main entrance. As he approached the basement door area, though, he saw another inmate named Lanier in the process of coming out through that door."

"Isn't Lanier the one who had a large and unexplained amount of cash in his room?"

"Yes. It looks like he was dealing happy dust to anyone who wanted to score it. So, seeing Lanier, Gardner had Lanier hold the door open and Gardner reentered that way. He went to the Supply Room, unlocked the door, went in, saw the body, came out in a hurry, and ran for help. Hurrying upstairs, he almost knocked the guard over, but by that time the guard already had word that something was up and he didn't stand around to listen to Gardner. He told Gardner to go to his room and Gardner did. That's the story."

"You sound unconvinced," Michaelson said.

"My clients pay me to prove their stories, Mr. Michaelson—not to believe them."

"As it happens, I do believe Gardner's story. Every word of it."

"That is your privilege."

"Your skepticism intrigues me," Michaelson said. "I realize that it's probably outside the scope of your instructions, but would you mind telling me why you balk at your client's account of things?"

"You're putting words in my mouth," Logan said.

"I certainly don't mean to be."

"Maybe it's just a difference in our ways of looking at things. To a trial lawyer defending a criminal case, what actually happened is a tactical parameter, not an absolute value. It isn't important for its own sake but because it's a practical limit on what you can expect a jury to believe. When Tony Martinelli was killed, for example, you were chatting with the warden at least a quarter of a mile away from the scene of the crime. Therefore, I can't very well base my trial strategy on convincing a jury that you might've killed Martinelli. For my purposes in defending Desmond Gardner, the fact that you didn't kill Martinelli, in and of itself, is completely irrelevant. What's relevant is the fact that I can't plausibly create a reasonable doubt by raising the possibility that you might have killed him."

"In other words, you don't make judgments about truth, only about provability."

"Right," Logan said.

"And you find Gardner's story unprovable."

"Right again."

"Why?"

"Is that a serious question?"

"Entirely serious."

"All right, I'll tell you. There is a locked room. A man was killed in that room. His death was recorded on videotape. Therefore, someone killed him."

"So far, it's safe to say we agree."

"Now comes the hard part. From and after the time Martinelli was killed, only one person came out of the Supply Room: Desmond Gardner."

"How do you know that?"

"Because I've been energetic enough to find out from my client and a couple of other sources the gist of what the videotapes show. If anyone besides Gardner had come out of the Supply Room, he either would have had to stay in the main basement corridor, in which case he would have shown up on the tape of that area, just as Gardner did; or he would have had to go up the back stairs to the first floor, in which case he would have been seen by the guard, Smith; or he would have had to go down the lateral hallway and out the basement door, in which case he would have been seen by Gardner."

"But Lanier did do exactly that—the third one, I mean. And Lanier has a background in computer technology."

"What's that got to do with anything?"

"I believe Warden Stevens told me that the videotape system is computer-controlled. Suppose Lanier got to, say, the computer work station in the B-4 Building Security Office, rigged a modem to communicate with the computers in the Central Administration Building, and instructed those computers to manipulate the videotape record."

"Those are neat concepts you're throwing around there, rigging modems and manipulating videotape records. There's a lotta nuts and bolts between theorizing about something like that and actually accomplishing it—assuming that it can be accomplished."

"I leave that in your more than capable hands," Michaelson said serenely. "In the State Department, I was always known as a big picture man. If I had a question about details, I sent a memo to the lawyers."

"Well, I have a problem with this big picture you're drawing: We can account for Lanier practically every relevant moment, and so we know he didn't go into the Supply Room, much less come out of it. He shows up on the basement video-tape pushing a wide dust mop down the basement corridor. He stops and tries to go in the Supply Room at one point, but the door is locked and he gives up. He pushes his dust mop some more, then heads down the lateral hallway. Between then and the point where he held the basement door open for Gardner, he couldn't have gone into the Supply Room because to do so he would have had to go back into the basement corridor and show up again on the videotape from the camera covering that area."

"How about before he ever shows up on the basement corridor tape in the first place?"

"I don't follow your question," Logan said.

"Let me ask you another one then. Where is the tape recording the images transmitted by the various video cameras physically kept? Each camera doesn't include its own tape, does it?"

"No. They aren't camcorders. They're essentially transmitters. The actual recording's done on a master video-tape-recorder in the central administration building."

"How? Physically, I mean. Is there an individual cassette for each camera or what?"

"No," Logan explained. "The transmissions are recorded on two continuous bands of six-inch tape on reel-to-reel spools—you know, like you sometimes see on old-fashioned main-frame computers. Each camera in the prison is electronically assigned a set of recording heads and an eight-minute segment of the tape on those spools. Whatever a given camera transmits is recorded on that camera's segment."

"And when the recording heads for one camera reach the end of that camera's segment, I take it, they automatically go back to the beginning of the segment and start recording over."

"Correct."

"Thereby erasing whatever has been recorded before."

"Correct again."

"It seems to me," Michaelson remarked mildly, as if he were thinking out loud rather than arguing, "that everyone has been making a rather critical assumption about the different videotapes."

"To wit," Logan prompted.

"To wit: that the tape retrieved for the Supply Room camera was running during the same eight-minute interval as the tape retrieved for all the other cameras."

"What alternative possibility is there?"

"That the Supply Room tape recorded Martinelli's shooting, and was then disabled, well before the other tapes began recording the segments that were frozen and retrieved. In other words, someone shot Martinelli and the Supply Room camera lens which thereupon stopped transmitting. Because it stopped transmitting, the video-taperecorder in the Administration Building stopped recording on the segment of tape for that camera. Because the video-taperecorder stopped recording, it stopped erasing."

"Damnation," Logan said. He sat up straight in his chair, then leaned forward. For the first time in the conversation his eyes showed a flicker of excitement. "Go on," he urged.

"Gladly. Let's see. We have Martinelli dead and the Supply Room camera disabled. The killer comes out of the Supply Room and goes about his business. His exit is of course recorded on the basement corridor camera. Exactly eight minutes later, however, that exit is erased, to be replaced by a recording of whatever is happening then—say, of Lanier dust mopping the basement corridor."

"That's great," Logan nearly shouted, his voice almost childish with delight. "Sonofabitch. That's really terrific. I can really do something with that."

"Glad to be of help," Michaelson said with a smile.

"Let's see, if—No." Logan's face instantly clouded over. "What's wrong?"

"No, it doesn't work. Your theory depends on the central

VCR no longer recording for the Supply Room camera once it's disabled."

"That's right."

"But it had to be recording."

"Why?"

"Because otherwise we would have had eight minutes of images on the Supply Room tape. What we had was the killing and then the rest of the tape taken up with snow. If the VCR had stopped recording, then the snow wouldn't have been recorded over whatever was on the tape before."

"My word," Michaelson acknowledged. "You're absolutely right. I'll have to think this through more thoroughly before I talk to the people at the Justice Department about it."

"No!" Logan bellowed.

"I beg your pardon?"

"Don't under any circumstances talk to anyone at the Justice Department about this. I don't want them to hear about this until the jury does."

"But you just said that. . . ."

"Exactly. As a matter of logic, your theory's a piece of shit. No offense. But the hole in your theory isn't obvious. It took someone as brilliant as me to spot it."

"Obvious or not, though, the hole's still there."

"Of course it is. But if I spring it on the feds by surprise, near the end of trial, they might not spot it until it's too late." Logan rubbed his hands together in gleeful anticipation. "Trial by ambush. I love it."

"You're overlooking something."

"What's that?"

"Securing Desmond Gardner's acquittal by fancy foot-work at trial still leaves Gardner in prison on the bribery conviction, at the mercy of the parole board. In his soul, he's the next thing to dead already. The only thing that's keeping him going is the hope of getting out of prison in time to rebuild a semblance of his life. If he ends up having to serve his full sentence for bribery, the acquittal you hope to secure on the murder charge will be a hollow victory."

"I think that the appropriate approach has to be one problem at a time," Logan said.

"That is your privilege."

"Anything else I can do for you?"

"There is one other area of inquiry, actually."

"What's that?"

"It relates to the bribery conviction. I understand that Gardner was videotaped by the FBI while accepting a bribe from someone to whom he gave an early copy of the mark-up version of a tax bill."

"That's right."

"In other words, he was set up."

"That's putting it mildly."

"Set up, presumably, with the help of the person who gave him the bribe."

"Not presumably. That one's a mortal certainty. No doubt about it, the guy was in bed with the feds on that little number from the word go. He set Gardner up and then he sold him out. I came down real hard on him during closing argument."

"A source, I'm certain, of infinite chagrin to the gentleman," Michaelson said. "But it brings us to the next question: Why did he do this?"

"To save his ass. Why else?"

"Can you possibly be a bit less generic?"

"The feds had the guy on hanky panky with a pension fund or some damn thing. So the guy says, 'I've had a United States Senator on my payroll for years, let's make a deal.' He hands 'em Gardner on a silver platter and gets off with restitution, a stiff fine, and ninety days on work release."

"I see. And what is this scoundrel's name?"

"Henry Gunderson. Chief executive officer of Gunderson Union Merchant Company in. . . ."

"Let me guess, New Orleans, Louisiana."

"How did you know that?"

"As I said," Michaelson smiled as he stood up, "I'm a big picture man. Good day."

CHAPTER 18

"Carrie," Marjorie said as she bustled past the central counter, straightening books on a remainder table as she went, "I hate to leave early, particularly on a night when you have an engagement yourself, but I really do barely have time to get home and get ready before Richard is supposed to pick me up."

Carrie offered her employer the gently mocking, tolerantly affectionate look that newly confident youth reserves for anxious middle age.

"This is the third time in the last twenty minutes that you've told me you don't have a minute to spare and must leave instanter. Please go. Kathy will be in by 5:30 and I'll have ample time to keep my appointment with McRobert Pond."

"You're right, of course." Marjorie stopped in her tracks. "I've been stalling because I'm rather puzzled and I guess a bit vexed at Wendy Gardner's sudden disappearance and continuing absence. I've been hoping that if I stalled long enough she'd find her way back in here."

"She's a big girl. She can take care of herself."

"In Washington, that is perhaps the epitome of *non sequitur*. You're certain that you didn't notice her leave?"

"Quite certain. Sorry. I just wasn't paying any attention to her."

"No reason you should have been." Marjorie walked back up to the serving platform and looked at the table where Wendy had been sitting. The only remaining evidence of her presence was the copy of *D.C. After Dark* she had been reading. "She was sitting here. I went to take Richard's phone call. I had my back turned for three minutes at most and in that interval she left in a very big hurry. Well, nothing to be done about it now."

Perhaps because it was the one remaining tangible link with Wendy that she had, Marjorie stuffed the newspaper into her purse and left in something of a hurry herself.

Although she was carrying three Woodward & Lothrop boxes in a generous plastic sack, Wendy strode toward the public phone with the natural grace of a born shopper. Reaching the phone, she set her purchases at her feet and then straddled them to deter the sneak thieves that her midwestern paranoia told her might be lurking nearby. The contents represented her clothing budget for roughly four months, and she didn't want somebody to make off with them.

She dialed the number and waited through a ring-and-a-half.

"Staff," a male voice said. "Randy Cox speaking."

"Hello, Randy," she said. "This is Wendy Gardner. What are you doing after work?"

CHAPTER 19

Jennifer Blair had once read a Washington novel in which a set piece Washington party given by a famous Washington hostess had played a key role. This novel had attributed the famous hostess's legendary success with Washington parties to her consummate skill in balancing guest lists: several important members of the congressional leadership, two or three big names from the cabinet, a representation from the Supreme Court and a sprinkling of diplomats—as if a Washington party was supposed to be a *tableau vivant* depicting The Separation of Powers. This had cured Jennifer Blair of reading Washington novels.

Jennifer Blair's intimate dinner parties—these days, only embassies and trade associations still had the time and resources to give grand parties in the traditional, thundering herd style—were intended to achieve particular objects. The object might be to improve the prospects of a bill pending in Congress, to speed the confirmation of a troublesome appointment, to win a coveted position for someone, to get a potential Presidential candidate taken seriously by the media or any of a variety of other desiderata that a State Department lobbyist like Charles Blair might have. Whatever the purpose, however, Ms. Blair knew that it was essential to focus on that object, to the exclusion of other concerns. This meant, among other things, that one of Jennifer Blair's dinner parties would never be confused with a pageant of the three branches of government.

The point of tonight's party, for example, was to see to it that an individual whom she detested on both political and personal grounds would be excluded from consideration for a major foreign policy post in the next administration. To accomplish this, her guest list had to include five elements:

(1) an alternative candidate—not someone who would get the job himself, necessarily, but someone who would be perceived as plausible competition for the person whose chances she wanted to ruin;

(2) a conduit to the likelier Presidential possibilities—a political operative rather than a substantive adviser;

(3) a resource person—someone with enough day-to-day contact with foreign policy to be able to provide accurate background information for any of her guests who were too lazy to do their own homework;

(4) a foil—a self-important fop who could be counted on to provide opportunities for the alternative candidate to say clever and occasionally profound things; and

(5) a syndicated columnist who would make the alternative candidate's status as an alternative candidate a matter of universal—that is to say, inside-the-beltway—knowledge.

Jennifer Blair had counted on McRobert Pond as the alternative candidate, and had therefore viewed his last-minute cancellation as a decidedly annoying development. Having

Richard Michaelson fall into her lap in the nick of time was a godsend that left Jennifer Blair feeling extremely pleased with herself. The more she thought about it, in fact, the more convinced she became that Michaelson would have been a better choice than Pond in the first place, and she wondered for a moment why she hadn't invited Michaelson to start with. Then, with a twinge of irritation, she remembered: because inviting him meant having that ass of a Marjorie Randolph tag along.

Oh well. One does what one must.

It was ten minutes until dinner. The columnist, the foil and the conduit were all in place, the first two with spouses and the third with a significant other. Ms. Blair had just slipped into the kitchen to check on the food and found that it was proceeding on schedule. She walked back into the living room and passed a little knot where the columnist, the conduit and the foil's spouse were conversing.

"Secretary of State?" the conduit said. "Do you think he'd take it?"

"I don't know," the columnist replied, nodding toward the door. "Let's ask him."

At this the conduit, the foil's spouse and Jennifer Blair all turned to watch Richard Michaelson and Marjorie Randolph walk into the room.

"What about it, Richard?" the columnist asked, loudly enough to be heard across the expanse of federal blue and Williamsburg green decor separating them. "If you were offered State in the next administration, would it be yes or no?"

Michaelson smiled at the columnist to acknowledge the question and stepped forward to greet Jennifer Blair and verify that she and Marjorie were acquainted. The columnist threw his head back to try to make his black, horn rimmed glasses scoot toward the bridge of his nose. Michaelson turned back toward the columnist-conduit-spouse knot.

"I make it a practice not to turn down jobs I haven't been offered yet," he said.

———

145

"Richard," the conduit remonstrated, "you're turning into a politician on us."

"It's contagious," Michaelson nodded.

Tallyho, Jennifer thought to herself, with considerable relief. Let the games begin.

". . . a risk that seems to me considerably overrated," the foil was saying while everybody else squirted lemon juice onto broiled swordfish. Detachment of western Europe from the Atlantic Alliance was the topic under discussion. "Wasn't it DeGaulle who said that the issue confronting France was whether it would remain France or become Poland?"

"Raymond Aron," the resource person said.

"Was that in his memoirs?" a significant other asked.

"*Le Spectateur Engagé*," the resource person answered, shaking his head.

"And if I'm remembering the reference correctly," Michaelson said, "he didn't suggest that the desirable answer to that question was the inevitable one."

"Let's come back down to earth," the foil said.

"Now that is in his memoirs," the significant other interjected. "Aron's, I mean. I remember it."

"To return to NATO," the foil persisted. "The United States has a conventional force in western Europe that is—what, a quarter-million men?"

"Three-hundred-five thousand, give or take the odd platoon," the resource person said. "That'll come down to two-hundred-twenty-five thousand if the Two-plus-Four agreement is ratified."

"At any rate, too large to be cheap but not nearly large enough to have a prayer of stopping the Red Army. What is its mission?"

"I think he's asking you," the columnist said to Michaelson.

"Its mission is to die trying," Michaelson said.

"Hello?" the foil responded. "Can you run that one by me again?"

"To be somewhat more precise," Michaelson continued, "the mission of the American troops stationed in Europe is to guarantee that the Red Army cannot advance without killing a significant number of U.S. soldiers."

"Thereby accomplishing what?"

"Thereby reassuring the Europeans that they are protected not only by U.S. troops but by U.S. missiles—the theory being that while we can't be counted on to put New York at risk to save Hamburg, we'd certainly do so to protect hundreds of thousands of American soldiers."

"Do you really think the Europeans believe that?" the foil asked. "Is there even a Soviet-Marxist threat for them to be concerned about any more?"

"The Russians have long since stopped being Marxists, and they may soon stop being Soviets. But they're not going to stop being Russians—and no one knows that better than the Europeans."

"That's the conventional wisdom, certainly," the foil said, by now clearly bluffing. "But ought we to rethink it? Especially now that the Berlin wall is a speed bump? It caught us flat-footed when it came down."

"As I recall," Michaelson said, "it also caught us flat-footed when it went up."

"So you seriously imagine that the Red Army will cross the Elbe if we withdraw our troops from Europe?"

"No, I don't," Michaelson said. "I don't think it will have to."

"As Napoleon once advised," the columnist remarked, "never try to kill someone who is in the process of committing suicide." He glanced at the foil as he said this, and the foil knew that he wasn't talking about western Europe.

* * *

147

Michaelson and Charles Blair hadn't exchanged a word during the meal, which had proceeded through appetizers, soup, salad and entree and was now careening recklessly toward dessert. Michaelson had given considerable thought to whether he should excuse himself before or after the strawberry schaum torte. Not without a pang, for he was very fond of German pastry, he concluded that it should be before.

He murmured an apology and rose from the table. He knew where the bathroom was. He walked upstairs, entered the bathroom, flushed the toilet, turned the cold water faucet on for three seconds, turned it off, and waited.

He had to wait four minutes before he heard Charles Blair's wary tread on the stairs. He listened as Blair reached the top of the stairs and walked down the hallway. He imagined Blair standing a few feet away from the bathroom door, gazing at it, wondering.

He heard Blair walk past the bathroom, then toward the bedrooms and the study at the end of the hall. Michaelson opened the bathroom door and stepped into the hallway himself. Blair turned around.

"I think we should talk right now, Charlie," Michaelson said. "I really do have to see them."

"How did you know I was the one who'd leaked them?" Blair asked. They were standing on either side of a desk in his study, looking at photocopies of a ship's manifest, a set of demurrage certificates, a bill of lading, a letter of credit, a warehouse receipt, and an eight-by-ten glossy photograph of a ship.

"I don't claim to be expert in the field," Michaelson answered, "but I have some notion of how lawyers write. As a class, they aren't given to specificity. When they serve a formal request for an array of precisely specified documents, one naturally suspects that they've gotten a hint beforehand about what to ask for."

"But they could have gotten the hint from anyone."

"Well, not just anyone. It had to be someone stationed in Washington at the time of the leak and who had some involvement with the subject matter of the leak."

"But that could have been a dozen people."

"It could have been five the way I calculated it," Michaelson said. "All five were wary—properly so, I might add. All five were reluctant to talk with me at all. All five took careful measures to cover themselves. Several of the five pretended that they didn't in fact know anything about the topic. But out of the five possibilities, only you went out of your way to steer me onto somebody else. Infallible evidence. Right out of the form book."

"Bravo." Blair beamed at Michaelson with professional appreciation. "Well done."

"Thanks and all that, but . . . ."

"It was the first time I'd ever done it. An unauthorized leak. I mean to another department of the government of course. You go to the press all the time with things, naturally."

"Naturally."

"It was just that I couldn't get over my disgust at the thing. It was so—so seedy, so pathetically tawdry. I passed it up the line in my own shop and when nothing happened I went ahead and let the cat out of the bag."

"Dropping a broad hint, if I'm not mistaken, not only to the Justice Department in Washington but to a U.S. Attorney out in the hinterlands."

"Right again. I knew that one might get squelched, but I thought there was no way they could kill two."

"Well, time will tell, I suppose," Michaelson said briskly. "Let's get to work, shall we?"

"You mean you don't see it?"

"A provocative question. Let's see: The merchant vessel *Cracow* sets sail from the Baltic with a cargo of golf carts, foodstuffs and lightweight clothing. After several stops it reaches the Caribbean, where it pays a call on Cuba. While at Cuba, it unburdens itself of the lightweight clothing and proceeds to

Tampico, Mexico. There, it takes on two hundred thousand metric tons of raw sugar, sold by Tracomex, the Trading Company of Mexico, through normal commercial facilities to a company identified as GUMCO, located in New Orleans. How am I doing so far?"

"I would say you're quite warm."

"GUMCO is of course the Gunderson Union Merchant Company."

"Correct."

"And so we come to the photograph." Michaelson studied the eight-by-ten glossy for several seconds. "In which we see the merchant vessel *Cracow* riding at anchor off Tampico."

"Right."

"Ah, I see. Riding rather low in the water."

"Quite low for a ship that was previously supposed to have unloaded all of its cargo, and was waiting to take on some sugar."

"Mm hmm. In other words, the United States of America unwittingly allowed the importation of two hundred thousand tons of Cuban sugar, upon the representation that it was actually Mexican sugar. The Mexican trading company didn't give the *Cracow* any sugar. All it gave the *Cracow* was a phony bill of lading to match a phony warehouse receipt."

"Both of which were specified in a quite real and perfectly negotiable letter of credit."

"And to accommodate this comic operaish and potentially rather embarrassing accidental subsidy of a hostile government, the Mexican sugar quota had to be raised substantially above the amount of sugar Mexico actually had available to sell to the United States."

"That is correct," Blair said.

"Which was done in Congress, I take it, and presumably done in exchange for valuable consideration of some kind."

"I know that it was done. The consideration you'll have to figure out for yourself."

"In other words, someone in a position of trust and con-

---

fidence in the Congress of the United States sold out his country."

"So it would appear."

Michaelson looked up. The joviality had faded from his face and there was no suggestion of banter left in his voice.

"You'll have to excuse me, Charlie. I've just become unaccountably anxious about the whereabouts of a young woman I met recently."

CHAPTER 20

Wendy was six feet from Randy Cox when she stepped into the doorway of the Palm Restaurant's taproom. She stood still for a moment, highlighted by the late sunlight that streamed through the doorway behind her. It was just after seven.

Wendy raised her hands to chin level and began, one finger at a time, to pull off the tight-fitting, black leather gloves she was wearing. She was in the midst of doing this when Cox turned from the bar toward the doorway and noticed her.

She heard his sharp intake of breath the moment he glimpsed her. He didn't try to conceal the impression she made on him. He stared, fascinated, almost reverent, unabashedly appraising and admiring her as he looked her over systematically from foot to head.

He began at her knee-length, black, saddle leather boots, moved up her legs to the close-fitting, British-Army-pipeclay-white slacks tucked into the boots, proceeded to the bright yellow men's cotton broadcloth button down shirt that deployed nicely around the gentle bulge of her breasts, noticed the gloves she was taking off and the black silk scarf around her neck, saw the gold pin—a pair of miniature spurs, joined together—highlighting the knot in the scarf, and finished by taking in her cool, fresh, naive, unspoiled, hard-as-marble, soft-as-silk nineteen-year-old face, framed by carefully combed blond hair.

"Well," Cox said, his voice slightly uncertain, "this is a Wendy I haven't seen before."

She strolled over to the bar, smiled briefly at Cox, and laid the now-removed gloves down on the mahogany.

"What are you drinking?" he asked.

"Seven and seven," Wendy said. Just like that. Like she came into bars and ordered uptown cocktails every night.

Cox nodded at the bartender, who glided away to fetch the drink. Cox took a sip from the gin and tonic in front of him.

"Don't be insulted," he said, "but I sort of thought of you as more the cheerleader type."

"I'm not insulted. I am a cheerleader. Or at least I was for a semester of my freshman year."

"No shit?"

"Well, a majorette, actually. If you watched the Badger game you probably saw me."

"Uh, 'badger game?' "

"My school's football game against the University of Wisconsin," Wendy explained, her eyes suggesting playfully that Cox could scarcely be trusted in the inner sanctum of Congress if he couldn't even keep the Big 10 straight. "It was on ESPN."

"Right," Cox said. "I must've been working that Saturday."

"Bull*shit*," Wendy said with a smile, coming down hard on the second syllable as she showed her teeth.

"Right again. So how's it going? What you're looking into I mean."

"I don't know." Wendy lowered her eyes briefly to show that she accepted the transition from banter to serious matters. "I don't really feel very comfortable with anything that's happened."

"That I can understand."

153

"I haven't been able to reach dad by phone. I think I'll drive out tomorrow and try to see him."

"With Michaelson?"

"I haven't decided about that part yet."

The bartender put Wendy's drink in front of her. Cox pushed some money at him. He took it and went away.

"Michaelson turned anything up yet?" Cox asked.

"It's hard to say. He seems to think he has."

"Seems to think?"

"It's all kind of hazy. He says he's found some things out, but when he explains what they are none of it makes much sense to me."

"There could be a reason for that."

"There could be a couple of reasons, I guess."

"There could at that," Cox said, pausing again to drink.

Wendy considered for a moment asking Cox for a cigarette. She decided not to. Clichés are one thing, she told herself, and pure cornpone is something else. She was trying to figure out some more satisfactory way to move things along, but she needn't have bothered. Cox was moving all by himself.

"Look," he said as he half turned to face her. "Tell me if I'm misreading the vibes here, but I don't think I am. Are you interested in me or am I just kidding myself? 'Cause I'm as interested as hell in you."

"Yeah," Wendy said. "*Interested* is the word all right."

"Okay," Cox said. "Okay." She noticed with satisfaction that he was nervous. "I have Seagram's Seven Crown in my apartment. I have Seven-Up in my apartment. I have everything required for safe sex in my apartment. Why don't we go there? Right now?"

"Ready when you are."

On 14th Street just beyond P in northwest Washington, someone in the mid sixties had built an eight-story apartment building of elephant-gray concrete. Had the building been conceived as a monument to European workers' housing it couldn't have been any more devoid of interest. It sat there, an oblong hulk with the shape and features of a grossly metastasized shoebox.

In the seventies, someone had affixed charcoal-gray brick facing—not brick, just brick facing—to the concrete on the street side of the building. This well meaning but misbegotten effort had changed the building from drab to ugly.

In the eighties, someone had attached gold-colored, perforated metal work to the middle third of the brick facing. This had changed the building from ugly to hideous.

It was on the eighth floor of this building that Randy Cox lived. As Wendy stepped into the elevator with him, she felt a little pang inside, a little blip behind her eyes, something that was half panic and half reality check.

One day during the summer she was fourteen, Wendy had stolen her mother's car keys, snuck out of the house, slipped behind the wheel of the sedan her mother had left parked on the street, put the key in the ignition, turned it, and heard the engine roar into life. Shifting the car into drive and taking her foot off the brake, she'd noted not without awe that she, all 103 pounds of her, was moving a couple of tons of machinery down the street. And that had been when she'd felt the little pang she felt again just now, compounded of equal parts "hey, this is really happening, it's not just something I'm dreaming about" and "what do I do now?".

No way around it, she was scared. No longer was she imagining it, no longer was she planning it, now she was doing it, and it frightened her. She gulped the fear back and went ahead.

The elevator door opened. Wendy and Cox stepped onto the eighth floor. The corridor was long and narrow. All of the doors were painted red. Cox used two keys to unlock a door about a quarter of the way down the hall. He stepped aside and she walked into his efficiency apartment.

On the wall above the convertible sofa, next to a Redskins pennant, she saw a poster of someone Spanish whom she didn't recognize (it was Che Guevara) being hit in the face with a custard pie. The poster's caption read, "Is Nothing Sacred?" She didn't get it.

Along the wall on the other side was the door to what Wendy surmised was the bathroom, followed by what looked like enough video and audio toys to account for one month's foreign trade deficit, including everything from a large-screen television to a compact disc player, all framed by two large speakers. The sleek, obviously expensive electronics contrasted sharply with the napkin-and-tumbler-littered coffee table shoved against one end of the sofa and the old-fashioned, round-topped refrigerator dominating nine square feet of linoleum masquerading as flagstones in the kitchen area.

A few feet from the door a personal computer precariously shared a card table with software, magazines and what looked to be at least two days' mail. A two-drawer mini-filing cabinet stood underneath the card table and seemed at first glance to be holding it up.

Wendy looked carefully around the room while Cox came in and walked over to a drink trolley near the card table. There was something missing and she couldn't put her finger on it. Telephone on the coffee table. *Washington Post*s piled up underneath the coffee table. Same for several days' editions of the *Washington Times*. Same for *Washington Monthly*. Same for three Sundays' worth of the *New York Times*. What wasn't there?

Books. She couldn't see a book in the place. Not even a handful of course books left over from college. Cox obviously read. He read voraciously. Like everyone in Washington, he was an information junkie. But he didn't read books. Last week's cover story and tomorrow morning's headline defined his horizons.

"It was seven and seven, wasn't it?" Cox asked as he lifted a decanter.

"Actually, I could use a chaser right now. Do you have a beer?"

156

"Possible, possible," Cox hummed, the soul of good humor.

He walked over to the refrigerator and opened it. From across the apartment it looked nearly empty. Crouching, he reached far in the back and emerged triumphantly with a can of Miller Lite.

He strolled back in her direction and handed her the can. Only at this point did it seem to occur to him that a glass might be called for. Rather than walk all the way back to the kitchenette, he scrounged a cocktail glass from the drink trolley and tendered this to Wendy.

"What are you majoring in?" he asked as he mixed a gin and tonic for himself.

"Primary Education." And my sign's capricorn, she thought. Get real.

"Gonna teach little kids, huh?"

"Maybe. I'm actually thinking more of administration, consulting, grant applications, that kind of thing."

He finished mixing his drink and smiled at her.

"The apple doesn't fall too far from the tree, I guess," he said.

"What's that mean?"

"Just that you're your father's daughter. And that's a compliment. Tunes?"

"Fine with me."

Cox walked over to the electronic array dominating the left wall. He turned on the preamp and the amplifier. He began to sort through the collection of compact discs.

I wonder what he'll pick? Wendy thought. Something classical to show me how sophisticated he is, *Bolero* or one of the other three things that people who never really listen to classical music have? Or some kind of rock, to show me how cool he is, even though he's almost twice my age?

Cox put a disc in the player. A moment later Wendy heard Christie Hynde singing "The Adultress." The Pretenders on compact disc. Like if you were listening to The Pretenders it would be this incredible tragedy to miss all these tonal nuances that you couldn't quite capture on a conventional record.

Cox had put down his drink to start the music. Now he took off his jacket and dropped it on one of the beanbags. He turned toward her. He loosened his tie and unbuttoned the top button of his shirt. Wendy wondered if she was supposed to find this unbelievably sexy. She guessed she was.

But then again, maybe not. Cox didn't really seem to think that the drinks or the music or the chat or the manner were sharpening her desire or creating an erotic mood or otherwise contributing to the business at hand. He seemed to be doing it more out of deference to social convention, the way you ask casual acquaintances how they are when you meet them.

"I went with someone in primary education for a few months last year," Cox said. Casually, making polite and innocuous conversation.

"No kidding." Wendy sipped the beer and with some effort avoided making a face. She could just barely stand Lite beer.

"Yeah. She was the educational psychologist at a K-4 school in Bethesda."

"*K-4*. She taught you the jargon, anyway."

Cox with what he took to be infinite finesse had in the course of this exchange moved to within twenty-two inches of Wendy.

"I thought the jargon was fabulous," he said. "You know what my favorite term from her was?"

"Tell me," Wendy said, shaking her head.

"Initiate play. Big problem in K-4 is kids who don't know how to initiate play in an appropriate way. I think maybe she wrote her Masters thesis on it."

"Initiating play in an appropriate way," Wendy repeated, looking directly into Cox's eyes and trying her damndest to seem fascinated. "It can be a problem even after fourth grade."

158

"I suppose it can," Cox said, smiling broadly. He took a long swig from his drink. "I have a question for you," he said then.

"What's that?"

"Do you do it with the lights on or off?"

"Yes," she said without blinking.

Wendy's legs were warm. Uncomfortably warm. Warm and sweaty and sticky.

It was the boots. She was naked except for the boots. Cox had asked her to put the boots back on after they'd both undressed, and she'd done it. Everything else made her feel tawdry, cheap, degraded, used, soiled—the boots made her feel ridiculous.

She lay quite still in the subdued lighting. She was lying underneath a baby blue blanket on a sheet and pillow that Cox had put down on the shag rug in front of his sofa. She had wondered when he was doing it why he didn't just open the couch out into a bed. Trying to imagine Bruce Willis or Beau Bridges doing that in a movie, though, she'd guessed she understood why Cox had regarded it as inappropriate to the occasion.

Next to her, Cox was breathing deeply and regularly, his eyes closed. She wondered if she dared.

By bending her neck at an uncomfortable angle, she could just see the digital clock next to the telephone. It was 8:42.

Prostituted himself. The phrase came back to her. At her father's sentencing hearing, the government lawyer had said that two or three times: Senator Gardner prostituted himself, he violated his sacred trust.

That lawyer knew what he was doing, she reflected. Those words cut. They sliced right through the skin, right down to the soul. She told herself that what she was doing wasn't the same thing, but that didn't make her feel okay about it.

———

159

With infinite caution, Wendy lifted her left arm. Cox stirred. Wendy froze, holding her arm still fifteen inches above the pillow.

Cox's regular breathing resumed. His eyes stayed closed. Wendy inched herself toward her edge of the rug, gradually pulling her body out from between the sheet and blanket.

There. She was out on the carpet. Keeping her eyes on Cox, she came up to a crouch. She got ready to back away, toward the card table.

"Wendy?" Cox mumbled.

She froze again. Cox's left arm reached over to where Wendy had been lying. His eyes half opened.

For a split second guilty fear paralyzed her. She fought the fear down, choked off the suddenly rising nausea, willed her voice to sound sultry and seductive again.

"Just looking for my gloves, tiger," she said.

"Gloves?"

She patted the area around her and came up with one of them. No matter how peremptorily she ordered herself to be calm, she couldn't take her eyes off him.

"Here we go," she said.

She climbed back under the blanket and whisked the glove back and forth across his nose and mouth. His eyes opened all the way.

"C'mere you insatiable minx," he murmured.

"You're quite certain she said nothing to indicate where she might be going?" Michaelson was asking Marjorie at 8:42.

"Naturally I am certain, Richard, or I wouldn't have spoken as I did." Marjorie was beginning to be vexed with her companion. They were in Michaelson's Omni, outside Hartnett Hall where they had just now discovered no evidence of Wendy Gardner.

"It's my fault," Michaelson muttered.

———————

"We are in complete agreement."

"Marjorie, I realize that my behavior must be exasperating. Please attribute that to my acute anxiety."

"Very well. Consider it attributed."

"And please humor me by allowing me to go over what we know that is pertinent to Ms. Gardner's whereabouts. She was sitting at a table reading."

"Correct."

"You came over to talk to her."

"Right."

"What did you talk about?"

"You."

"Me?" Michaelson said. "Nothing true, I trust?"

"Do stay to the point, Richard. She said you weren't very nice. I defended you ably and effectively without, however, imputing niceness to you. At the conclusion of this conversation, she seemed quite noncommittal."

"Very well. You were then called to the phone to talk with me."

"Correct."

"The conversation lasted only a short time as I recall."

"A relatively short time."

"And when you looked back she had gone and appeared to have departed in some haste."

"Correct again."

"Is there any chance that anyone could have talked to her during the interval between the time you left her and the time you noticed she was gone?"

"I consider that very unlikely. The store was practically empty. Anyone coming in would certainly have attracted my attention and Carrie's."

"So," Michaelson mused, more to himself than to Marjorie, "she thought of something. Heard something. Overheard something. Read something."

"Scratch heard and overheard. The only conversation

during the interval was the one I was having with you over the telephone, and Wendy couldn't have heard any part of that."

"And scratch thought of something, too," Richard said. "Why?"

"Because we can't do anything useful with it. That leaves the possibility that she read something while you were on the phone—read something rather galvanic. You said she was reading while she was sitting at the table. What was she reading?"

"*D.C. After Dark,* that semi-underground newspaper."

"You're certain of that?"

"Richard, someday you are going to ask that question once too often. I have it with me because I gathered up what she left at the table, and the timing of this little improvised evening out with you was so tight that I barely had time to change clothes and just had to dump the contents of one handbag into another when I exchanged purses."

"May I see the tabloid in question, Marjorie?"

"Certainly, Richard."

She dug the paper out of her purse and barely restrained herself from dropping it in his lap. He turned on the car's dome light.

"Something in here set her off on whatever it is she went off on."

"So it would appear," Marjorie agreed.

"I suppose there's nothing to do but look through it ourselves and see if we can figure out whatever it was."

"You read the left hand pages," Marjorie said, "and I'll read the right hand pages."

It looks like that one did it, Wendy thought. Cox was snoring like a water buffalo in the depths of hibernation. It was 9:01.

She slipped out from under the blanket. The sonorous rumbling from Cox's nose and throat continued. Wendy found

162

her shirt and panties and picked them up. Those she could put back on without taking the boots off. Removing the boots seemed like a noisy, time-consuming procedure that she couldn't allow herself. At the same time, she didn't intend to go buck naked through Cox's files.

Pantied, shirted and still shod, she crept over to the card table. Every three seconds or so, she glanced backward over her shoulder at Cox's sleeping, snoring form. The snores were deep and reassuring.

Kneeling at the card table, she delicately opened the top drawer of the filing cabinet. She did this by inches. Each inch produced a grating squeak and at every other squeak she glanced over her shoulder. But the snores continued.

She got the drawer open to about half its length. She found the first document inside and pulled it up to where she could read it in the half light: VCR Owner's Manual. She let it drop, found the next item and lifted it up: bank statement from two months ago. Her spirits sinking a bit, she started to go through the drawer's contents more quickly: student loan papers; copies of income tax returns; warranty cards; lease; more owner's manuals; copy of the promissory note on his current car loan; drafts of two articles he had written, with rejection letters from *The New Republic, The Atlantic,* and *The American Spectator;* more bank statements; a box of cancelled checks; a box of check pads.

That was it for the first drawer. Wendy chewed contemplatively on her lip. She glanced at her coital partner, still obliviously snoring.

Wendy didn't see how she could possibly be wrong. Something had to be here. She sighed, slipped the first drawer shut, and began to open the second.

Average reading speed for high-level officials in Washington is one thousand words per minute. The average for bookstore owners in that impatient city is somewhat higher. Michaelson and Marjorie had gotten through four pages of concert listings, night spot reviews, record reviews, restaurant reviews and columns of bilious opinion without spending very much time at it but also without picking up any hint as to where Wendy Gardner might be.

Michaelson turned the page. This brought to view the first two pages of a very long article titled, "Half-Staff Blues: Woes of a Part-time Congressional Staffer in Lotus Land East."

"This looks more promising," Michaelson said. He and Marjorie set to reading it with renewed avidity. Michaelson's assessment, however, proved optimistic, for the article turned out to be nothing more exciting than the selfabsorbed chronicles of a a highly libidinous aide who found it frustrating that what the taxpayers paid him to do so often interfered with his bedding of a platoon of young women who, according to him, desired him more than anything except a grade-and-step pay increase.

"I don't see anything very helpful there," Marjorie said. "Nor do I."

He turned the page. Michaelson made short work of a profile of a local heavy metal group that was trying to find a label, which Michaelson learned meant a recording company; while Marjorie quickly digested an article on people who ripped off videotape sellers by bootlegging unauthorized copies.

"Serves them right for discouraging reading," she sniffed.

Michaelson turned the page again. He came to a two-page spread continuing and concluding the Half-Staff Blues article. They read speedily and fruitlessly through that.

Michaelson turned the page again. And groaned slightly. The reviews and articles had given way to classified advertisements in tiny type.

"We seem to have reached the personals, as lonely hearts ads are called these days," Marjorie said. "Any ideas?"

"Only one," Michaelson answered, sighing. "Let's read them."

*   *   *

Wendy finished her inventory of the second file drawer. For the most part, it was more of what she'd found in the first drawer, plus some blank stationery, legal pads and ballpoint pens.

She did find a letter-size envelope with twenty-three one hundred dollar bills in it, and remembering that inmate Lanier had also had a large amount of cash on hand she spent a few seconds pondering the hypothesis that Cox sold dope. She concluded that this didn't really get her anywhere by itself and besides, it wasn't really what she was looking for. She needed something more.

She sat gingerly on the carpet. She was baffled. There wasn't anyplace else in the apartment to look. Not for what she was seeking. There wasn't any bedroom, she'd already been in the bathroom and there wasn't anyplace in there to keep it anyway, she couldn't imagine it being in the closet that he had casually opened in her presence. The only possible place was here, in the filing cabinet under the computer.

Computer.

She raised her eyes to the personal computer on the card table. She thumped her forehead with the heel of her right hand.

Schmuck, she said to herself, cheerfully ignorant of the actual meaning of this word.

She rose, sat down on the chair in front of the card table, and began to look through the software. The chore absorbed her. She was sure that it wouldn't be long now.

Wendy turned on the computer and the monitor. This produced a disconcerting beep and Wendy jumped, glancing anxiously over her shoulder as she did so. Cox snored reassuringly on.

Among the software, Wendy had found a boxed three-ring binder labeled Office Manager. She booted the FileIt disk and ordered the computer to list its contents. After an interval of whirring and clicking the screen showed:

---

1. RNB   2. HLT   3. PRT   4. LEB

5. JDQ   6. DSG   7. DTT   8. MLG

9. CDR   10. JRH   11. REF   12. KLH

"Shit," she breathed. "He didn't even bother to code it."
She told the computer to retrieve file 6. Whirrs and clicks.
Then the screen filled with type. At the top of the screen, flush
left and all caps, was the heading DESMOND S. GARDNER.

"SWM," Michaelson read. "Forgive my obtuseness, but this
isn't really my area. What does SWM mean?"

"Single white male," Marjorie translated. "B/D means
bondage and discipline, S/M means slave and master, golden
shower refers to a sexual fetish I'd just as soon not discuss,
thank you very much, generous means the advertiser expects
to pay or to be paid by the respondent, depending on which
party the adjective refers to, no pros means the opposite."

"All right. Thank you. 'Single white male seeks WF'—
that would be white female, I take it?"

"You take it correctly."

"Good. '—seeks white female for cool whip/mayonnaise
party.' Cool whip/mayonnaise is obviously jargon. What does
it mean?"

"I'm not certain, but I suspect that part is literal."

"You mean this fellow wants someone who will allow him
to cover her with . . ."

"Yes."

"Hm. 'Non-smokers only.' Remarkably fastidious under
the circumstances."

Once you knew the code, Michaelson reflected, you could
read these things very quickly indeed. He sped through four

166

columns of them in no time and was starting the fifth when Marjorie identified the essential problem.

"The more of these I read," she said, "the clearer it becomes to me that I don't have the faintest idea of what I'm looking for."

"I share your perplexity. I can only hope that whatever it is will be so obvious that we'll know it the moment we see it."

"That seems unlikely."

"Bingo," Michaelson said.

"What does that mean?"

"It means that you stand refuted by experience. Immediate experience in this case." He pointed to an ad three quarters of the way down the fifth column.

"Wanna horse around?" Marjorie read. " 'I have just what it takes to spur you on. WF will give free rein to your most unbridled fantasies—and your bridled ones too. If you're ready to pony up, write Diana at Box 3096. Photo $5/SASE.' She even expects you to pay your own postage. Frankly, Richard, this is a side of you I hadn't suspected."

"Three oh nine six is the numeral written beneath the picture of a fetching young woman in riding costume that was found—I refer, of course, to the picture, not the young woman herself—in Sweet Tony Martinelli's quarters the afternoon he was shot to death."

"I see. In other words, working on your assumption that the number underneath the picture was part of a telephone number, Wendy may well have spent the better part of today running down a blind alley."

"Correct," Michaelson said.

"Then she saw the number in here, put it together with what the picture actually showed, and leaped to the conclusion that the number had an entirely different significance."

"Correct."

"Causing her to go racing off to—where?"

"I'm not certain," Michaelson said. "But I think the next place we should look is the address on the subscriber's mailing label on this newspaper."

"November 19th," Wendy read silently from the screen. "Check received from Gunderson. No indication of other mail, telephone or personal contact. Nothing done or requested in connection with check.

"November 26th: Check received . . . ."

Wendy suddenly stopped reading and sat up straight. Something was wrong. What was it?

She couldn't hear snoring anymore, that's what.

She looked over to the makeshift bed in front of the sofa. Cox wasn't there.

All at once the hard rock sound of The Who blared through the apartment at ear-splitting level. Wendy jumped in her seat. She looked over at the stereo equipment. Cox was standing there, naked. He was holding in his right hand a heavy, copper-colored paperweight, molded to resemble parchment and engraved with the first words of the Constitution. In his left hand he was holding the envelope she'd snatched from his desk to write down Jeff Logan's phone number—the envelope addressed to Diana at Post Office Box 3096. He started to walk toward her.

Wendy jumped out of the chair and swiveled around to face him head on.

"I'll scream," she shouted at him.

Half smiling, he jerked his head toward the stereo.

"Scientifically certified to be the world's loudest rock band," he said. "Go ahead and scream. No one'll be able to hear you. Even if they do, they'll think it's part of the music."

He stopped three feet away from her and waited for a moment to let the hopelessness of her situation sink in.

"You know what, Wendy?" he said. "You're going to bimbo heaven."

168

CHAPTER 21

Wendy kicked at Cox with her left leg. A politician's daughter, she aimed the kick at his testicles. Cox blocked her foot before it could get near that vulnerable territory, but the heavy leather boot she was still wearing jolted him all the same, even though it only slammed into his forearm and thigh. He staggered backward a step.

Using the instant's respite to dash for the door, Wendy got the first bolt thrown but heard Cox coming up behind her before she could reach the second. Cox's left hand slammed into the door a heartbeat after Wendy darted away from it.

She scampered toward the couch. Warier now, Cox turned and slowly closed the distance between them. Wendy's head fake toward the kitchenette threw Cox off balance for a moment but he recovered before she could skitter past him. Reversing the false start, she jumped to the couch. His face glistening, Cox turned and looked up at her, now about six feet away from him.

"This is pointless, Wendy." He didn't sound winded yet. "You're just going to get yourself hurt worse than you have to."

"You come one step closer and we'll see who gets hurt." The brave words sounded hollow to her but Cox, who had started to move toward her again, hesitated.

"You stinking little informer," Wendy spat at him. "You miserable, low life—" She paused a moment, for her inventory of epithets wasn't particularly well stocked. "weenie," she finished then, less than triumphantly.

"*Informer?*" Cox demanded.

"You set my father up. Then you sold him out to the feds. Now you're helping the government kill him to shut him up."

"Wendy," Cox said, "one of us is confused. If I were working with the government, I'd hardly have to kill you over what you saw here tonight, would I? And if the government for some reason wanted to kill the Senator, whom it has conveniently tucked away in prison, why would it need my help?"

Certainty evaporated from Wendy's face. Satisfactory answers to these questions didn't come instantly to mind.

"If your I.Q. were twenty-five points higher," Cox said then, "you'd be dangerous." He started toward her again.

A harsh rasp cut through The Who. Cox glanced toward the door. Someone was buzzing his apartment from downstairs. Wendy leaped feet first from the couch directly at Cox. She got the sole of one boot on his face and the sole of the other on his chest, knocking him down and sprawling near him. Something hard pressed her head. She grabbed it—it was one of Cox's shoes—and hurled it at the tiny window near the kitchenette. It missed by eight inches. Scrambling to her feet, she hurried toward the buzzer.

Downstairs, Michaelson pushed the white button opposite the name R. Cox a second time. He waited for another long moment while nothing happened, then glanced at Marjorie.

"Looks like no one's home," he said, his voice disappointed and frustrated.

Then there was a yawp from the speaker in the entryway where they were standing.

"Help!" a female voice that was almost drowned out by

170

insanely loud rock music said. Nothing else came over the speaker, and the buzz that would open the inside door didn't come.

"Hey!" Michaelson yelled as he began pounding on the inside door, trying to attract the attention of the guard at the security desk inside. Marjorie, better schooled in the lessons of detective novels, simply began pushing every doorbell in the entryway.

This is it, Wendy thought as Cox slapped her full on the face with his open palm, driving her away from the buzzer/speaker. He's got me. Falling heavily to the floor, she felt blood flowing from the inside of her cheek and cursed herself for not thinking fast enough to just buzz in whoever it was without bothering to talk to them.

Cox stood over her, straddling her, awkward in his nakedness because of the care he was taking to guard his scrotum. She waited for the paperweight to fall and for her world to go black forever.

It didn't fall. Instead, he reached down with his left hand and backhanded her across the face. She yelped with pain and saw white and red flares go off behind her eyes. Only then, after he was sure she was stunned and his loins were safe, did Cox raise the paperweight.

Tougher than Cox gave her credit for, Wendy spread her legs apart as fast and as hard as she could. Cox's feet flew out from under him and he toppled backward to the floor. The paperweight flew from his right hand.

Wendy bounded to her feet and pounced on the heavy piece of copper, which had skidded several feet across the carpet. With designs on braining Cox with it, she turned and raised it. Cox was also on his feet by now, though, and she thought it the better part of prudence to retreat. Brandishing the paperweight as fearsomely as she could manage, she fell back to the area just in front of the couch.

Cox kept his distance, standing by the computer, more or less directly across the apartment from her.

"You should see yourself," he said. "That head has to be hurting."

"It is," she nodded. "But it's still in one piece."

"Those people downstairs aren't going to help you, whoever they are," he continued. "Probably just cranks anyway. Even if they're not, the guard won't let them past."

"They'll still know that a woman called for help from this apartment."

"Chance I'll have to take," Cox said. "You have to understand something. I'm not going to prison. I'm not going to spend the next five years afraid to bend over in the shower."

"Well I'm real sorry for whatever inconvenience it causes you," Wendy sputtered, "but I'm just going to have to do my best to stay alive."

"It's pointless, Wendy. Look, if those people downstairs were going to help, they'd be here by now. This is a small apartment. I'm bigger and stronger than you are. It's just a question of time. Sooner or later I'm going to get you and we're going to do what we have to do. The only question is whether you're going to get the shit kicked out of you first."

The presumption infuriated her. She didn't blame him for calling her a bimbo. She'd earned that one. Treating her like a wimp, though, like someone who'd go docilely to slaughter just to avoid getting punched too hard in the meantime—that left her livid with rage. From the rage she drew inspiration for an effort at verbal abuse less insipid than her last one.

"We'll see who kicks the shit out of who, you arrogant asshole," she shouted. "I don't know if you've noticed, you tweedy little buffoon, but I'm the one that's winning this fight so far." In a paroxysm of righteous anger, she wound up and threw the paperweight as hard as she could directly at Cox's head.

Cox dove to the floor. The Constitution paperweight flew past him and smashed through the screen on his computer.

Downstairs, meanwhile, Michaelson and Marjorie were preparing to confront the apartment's security guard, who was

---

172

running toward the lobby door without offering any evidence of cooperative intentions. He turned a lever lock and jerked the door open.

"Let me explain," Michaelson said rapidly.

"You're creating a disturbance," the guard said simultaneously, "and you'll have to—" He stopped in mid threat. His mouth opened. "Mr. Michaelson," he said then. "I haven't seen you for over ten years."

"What a pleasant surprise," Michaelson said, managing a smile. "Marjorie, allow me to introduce Lance Corporal Walter Sedgwick, United States Marine Corps, late of the security detail responsible for a near eastern embassy that I had the honor to serve in as deputy chief of mission. Corporal Sedgwick, Ms. Marjorie Randolph, of the Virginia Randolphs, proprietress of what is far and away the best bookstore in Washington."

Sedgwick seemed unsure whether to salute or shake hands, his confusion compounded by the fact that the can of Mace he had pulled from his belt and was still holding would have complicated either activity.

"We heard a woman call for help from Room 814," Michaelson said. "Perhaps in view of the urgency of the situation we could cut the formalities short and proceed directly there."

"Yessir," Sedgwick responded. He admitted them and set off at a run for the elevators.

In Cox's apartment, meanwhile, the protagonists had clinched but it wasn't altogether clear who had caught whom. Cox was indeed bigger and stronger than Wendy, which gave the punches he was landing on her rib cage telling effect. On the other hand, Wendy's teeth were harder than his right ear lobe, which was now between them and would soon be perforated by them. He pinned both of her arms with one of his and he periodically lifted her off the ground, but this didn't keep her from flailing with her knees and feet, to the acute disadvantage of his shins and thighs.

When Sedgwick opened the door, his first thought was

that the couple before him was dancing, in pretty much the usual way, to the overture from the rock opera *Tommy* that was at the moment blaring from two speakers in the apartment. A second glance, however, convinced him that the situation was more serious.

"All right!" he barked in tones that easily overrode the music. "That's enough!"

Michaelson stepped into the room, crossed to the stereo equipment, and turned the amplifier off. The sudden absence of noise was for a moment startling.

"He threatened to kill me," Wendy said.

"I can explain," Cox said.

"What a sight this place is," Marjorie said.

"I'd better call the police," Sedgwick said.

"Wait a minute," Michaelson said. "Please."

Everyone looked at him, as if sobered by the injection of civility. "Corporal Sedgwick, I would appreciate it very much if you would hold off on calling the police for the moment. Marjorie, would you please escort Ms. Gardner to the bathroom and help her into something more suitable to the circumstances. Mr. Cox, you and I have some talking to do, and we have to do it very quickly."

"When are you going to let me out?" Wendy demanded of Marjorie ten minutes later when she was still closed in the bathroom.

"As soon as I get these last little bits of ear lobe out from between your front teeth, dear. Young ladies of your station shouldn't go about with human flesh between their teeth."

"Would someone at least tell me what's going on? I deserve that much."

"If I gave you what you deserve, *cherie*," Marjorie said matter of factly, "you wouldn't sit down for a week. Fortunately for both of us, I have neither the authority nor the energy for such an ambitious undertaking. But don't press me too far."

"Mr. Cox," Michaelson was saying at about the same time, "you are going to prison. You can go to prison for the nonviolent crime of corruption in office, or you can go to prison for kidnapping, attempted murder and whatever the legal term for beating a woman half your size is. I leave it to you to decide which of these alternatives is likely to have less insalubrious consequences for you."

"What are you getting at?"

"I want to walk out of here with all the knowledge and documentary information you have concerning compromising relations between an individual named Gunderson and persons associated in any way with the United States Congress. In exchange, I will give you until 1:30 tomorrow afternoon before I report what I know to the authorities. I suggest that you use the time not for flight but to consult an attorney, have him get in touch with the appropriate government personnel, and cut the best deal he can for you. If you come across with everything you know, I will try to persuade Ms. Gardner not to press charges on the basis of tonight's activities."

"How much time do I have to think it over?"

The bathroom door opened. Marjorie and Wendy came out.

"None," Michaelson said. "Yes or no."

"You win," Cox sighed.

It didn't take long. Forty-five minutes later, Michaelson, Wendy and Marjorie were back in the lobby, where Sedgwick had promised them a reasonably private telephone.

"Who do you want to call?" Wendy asked.

"Stevens," Michaelson said. "We need Billikin's cooperation in the long run, but we need Stevens's cooperation in the next twelve hours. The operative principle is first things first."

"Why is Stevens going to cooperate with us?"

"Mr. Stevens is going to cooperate," Marjorie explained primly, "because by cooperating he is going to get an opportunity to shove the solution to this crime down the collective throat of the Federal Bureau of Investigation, and make them like it."

"Precisely," Michaelson said.

CHAPTER 22

"A long-standing tradition of the American civil service holds that briefings should always consist of exactly three points," Michaelson said. "At today's meeting, I have to depart from that rule, as I have only two points to make."

"Perhaps you could make them then," Warden F. Whitmore Stevens said.

Michaelson glanced around the small assembly gathered in the basement of Honor Cottage B-4 at Fritchieburg. In addition to Stevens and himself, those present included Clark Grissom, the head of the FBI team investigating Martinelli's murder, Correctional Officer Grade-2 Wesson Smith, and Martin Billikin from the Justice Department's White Collar Crime office. Adding to the oddity of the venue was the presence of a portable video-taperecorder and monitor. It was about one o'clock in the afternoon, some fifteen hours after Wendy's struggle with Cox. None of the inmates was in evidence.

"Well, I can state the points at least," Michaelson said in response to Stevens's suggestion. "Making them may prove to be a bit of a challenge."

"I'll say," Grissom muttered.

"My points are these," Michaelson continued placidly. "One, that Desmond Gardner didn't kill Sweet Tony Martinelli; and two, that the investigative resources that have thus far been devoted to trying to prove that he did should therefore be diverted from that unpromising objective to the more fruitful one of trying to discover why Martinelli was killed."

"Not who did kill him, but why he was killed?" Grissom demanded.

"That is correct. We already know who did it. The interesting question is why."

"I can't wait to hear this," Billikin said.

"I think it's only fair to tell you," Grissom interjected, speaking to Michaelson, "that as far as I'm concerned you've got a tough row to hoe. Facts are facts."

"It's hard to argue with tautologies," Michaelson acknowledged.

"I know all about that little adventure last night with that Cox character, and I can guarantee you that's going to bear some looking into—from several points of view. But I don't see any solid connection between that guy and the Martinelli killing."

"There is in my judgment a substantial connection," Michaelson insisted. "We can start . . . ."

"This is a digression," Stevens objected. "You said your first point was, Gardner didn't do it. Let's get to that. If we're still with you when you're through making your pitch on that issue, we can talk about this other stuff."

"Entirely right," Michaelson conceded. "Let me begin by asking this question: What theory do you have to account for the gun that killed Martinelli being successfully smuggled into the building?"

"We have to speculate," the FBI agent conceded. "The most logical possibility is that it was smuggled in disassembled, with each piece too small to set off the metal detector."

"I see," Michaelson said. "Not a promising theory, if my own experience and Officer Smith's assurances about the capabilities of the window metal detector are any guide. But, assuming you're right, we approach the critical point."

He gestured toward a small, wooden table that had been set up in the intersection of the corridor and the lateral hallway. A blue cotton cloth covered the table. Arrayed on the cloth were a .22 caliber Colt Targetmaster pistol, a red and white box of Remington .22 caliber long rifle ammunition, and a pair of blue and white cotton work gloves.

"Warden Stevens has kindly supplied the ammunition," Michaelson said. "Can we agree that the other items are those found in the Supply Room along with Mr. Martinelli's body?"

"Those're my initials on the evidence bag tags, and I took 'em out of the bags myself," Grissom said.

"Good. Now, Officer Smith, I imagine you have some substantial familiarity with firearms."

"Sure," Smith said.

"How is that particular weapon loaded?"

"It's clip-fed," Smith answered instantly. "There's a magazine, called a clip, inside the handle. There's a spring inside the magazine. You put the cartridges into the clip, put the clip into the handle, then pull that slide on top of the gun back to load the first cartridge into the breech. After you do that, the action of firing the gun automatically ejects the spent shell casing and loads the next cartridge from the clip into the breech."

"Perhaps you could show us," Michaelson prompted. "About loading the clip, I mean. The rest we can leave for the moment to our collective imaginations."

Smith glanced at Stevens, who nodded briefly. Smith walked over to the table and picked up the pistol. He checked to make sure that the safety was on. He pulled the slide back to make sure that there were no bullets in the gun. He pushed a button above the trigger guard. A vented black metal rectangle snapped about three inches out of the bottom of the handle. Smith pulled this object completely free of the gun and laid the pistol itself down.

"That, I take it, is the clip?" Michaelson asked innocently.

"Right," Smith said, his voice a bit distracted. "You want me to load this now?"

"Yes," Michaelson said.

Smith opened the box of ammunition. The cartridges seemed remarkably small—no more than an inch long and at most a quarter-inch in diameter at the base. Smith gripped the clip in his left hand and picked up one of the cartridges between the thumb and index finger of his right.

"One moment, Officer Smith," Michaelson said. "Excuse me. I forgot to mention that I'd like you to load the weapon while wearing those gloves."

"What?" Smith demanded, his face an expressive depiction of bald astonishment. "Are you serious?"

"Quite serious. Those cotton work gloves there. Please put those on and then load the cartridges into the clip."

"I couldn't do that in a million years," Smith snorted. "Neither could anyone else."

"Do me a favor. Try."

Smith tried. The effort amply confirmed his assertion of impossibility. His last attempt ended with the clip's spring sending a very much unloaded bullet spinning up into the air.

Michaelson caught the cartridge before it could fall back to the table.

"No sense taking chances, eh?" he said, smiling at the others. "What a loss to American law enforcement if it got us all."

Smith reached for another cartridge.

"Wait a minute," Stevens ordered.

"Yes, do wait," Michaelson said. "I don't think we require further demonstration. I suspect that Officer Smith here is the most proficient among us in this particular area, but I'm willing to have anyone else who cares to try take a stab at it. I'm confident that the results will be the same. I will pay one thousand dollars to anyone here who can load a .22 caliber cartridge into that clip while wearing that pair of cotton work gloves."

"Proving what?" Grissom asked.

"That it can't be done. It's perfectly possible to fire a gun while wearing gloves. Loading a small-caliber, clip-fed weapon while wearing thick, awkward gloves like these is a different matter."

"So what?"

"So," Michaelson said musingly, "if the gun were smuggled into the building in pieces and assembled—and therefore loaded—in here, there should either have been fingerprints on the shell casing found in the Supply Room, or there should have been some explanation other than those work gloves for the absence of such prints."

"All right," Billikin said with a shrug. "There was some other explanation."

"For example?" Michaelson prompted.

"For example, whoever loaded the gun did it bare-fingered and then wiped the prints off."

"Wiped them off how? Once they're in the clip you can't reach them anymore."

"True enough," Grissom said. "But after you've fired the gun it ejects the spent shell casing. Then you can pick it up and wipe it off very easily."

"But in that case, there should have been prints on the bullets that were still in the clip," Michaelson insisted. "And there weren't. Were there?"

Grissom's response was a grudging shake of his head.

"He's got you there," Billikin said, a trace of irony in his voice.

"He's got both of us there," Grissom rejoined. "It was your theory."

"Okay," Billikin said. "Fair enough. Scratch one theory. So someone loaded the gun wearing surgical gloves instead of those work gloves."

"And then I suppose," Michaelson said, "whoever this was must have concealed the surgical gloves so cleverly that a top-notch scene-of-crime team from the FBI's Washington Field

181

Office failed to turn them up during an exhaustive search of the premises and surrounding area. Doesn't seem likely, does it?"

"No it doesn't," Grissom said emphatically.

"The gun could have been loaded and concealed in the cottage two weeks ago, and the surgical gloves smuggled clear out of the prison before the murder ever took place," Billikin said.

"Bit of a stretch, isn't it?" Michaelson asked tolerantly. "Surely someone who had planned a murder that meticulously would have contrived to do the actual killing in such a way that he wouldn't have been videotaped entering and then running out of the murder room around the time the fatal shot was fired. Or don't you agree?"

"Something Gardner planned on could've gone wrong and upset his plans," Billikin persisted.

"That's one possibility. Another possibility, though, is that a key piece of physical evidence is inconsistent with the hypothesis of Gardner's guilt."

"It's a hell of a reach from that fact to where you want to go with it," Grissom said.

"Isn't it true," Michaelson asked the man, "that criminals frequently overlook the possibility of fingerprints on bullets, as opposed to weapons, that shell casings are ideal receptacles for prints, and that wrongdoers are not infrequently convicted on the basis of prints found on cartridges and shell casings even though the perpetrators had wiped the weapons themselves clean?"

"Yes it is," Grissom said. "But it's also true that there's absolutely nothing inevitable about finding a fingerprint on any surface, ever. Half of what fingerprint experts do is explain to juries why no prints were found in such and such a place."

"I defer to your technical expertise," Michaelson nodded. "But the point troubled you in this case from the beginning, didn't it? Isn't that one of the reasons that you felt you didn't have enough of a case yet to charge former Senator Gardner?"

"That's within the Bureau," Grissom said, but the answer to Michaelson's question was clear from his face.

"And of course added to that are some other troubling questions: How did Gardner, in the few seconds the videotape record allowed to him after entering the room, come up with the gun, surprise Martinelli, kill him with an expert shot, disable the camera, discard the gun, take off the gloves and get rid of them too? Why did Martinelli, having entered a room that he had no right to be in, for a purpose presumably criminal, stand in full view of the surveillance camera and as far as possible from the door, when his normal instinct would have been to stand directly beneath the camera and as close as possible to the door? And in some ways most interesting, how and why did the killer stop the transmission from the surveillance camera only considerably after disabling the camera itself?"

"Yeah, sure," Grissom said. "You're right. That stuff bothers me. I can really see a slick shyster play it up, and I can definitely see a jury not buying the case."

"Nevertheless . . . ." Michaelson prompted, smiling.

"Nevertheless is right. The fact remains that this guy Martinelli nevertheless got dead inside that room at a particular time, and the only other person who could possibly have been in that room anywhere near that time is this scumbag politician, Gardner. Martinelli was killed by somebody who was in the room with him. Gardner was. Nobody else was. Nobody else went into the room. Nobody else came out of the room. Nobody else was still in the room. Therefore and nevertheless, Gardner killed the sonofabitch. The problem isn't figuring it out, the problem is proving it."

"Your syllogism is correct in the formal sense," Michaelson said. "Like all syllogisms, however, it's no stronger than its major premise—and as to that premise I have come to entertain the gravest doubts."

"I'm not sure what you're saying, but I think you're trying to tell me I'm wrong."

"Perhaps if I had Ms. Gardner's assistance I could explain

the matter more clearly. Wendy?" Michaelson called. "Are you back there somewhere?"

Wendy stepped out of the stairwell at the back of the corridor and walked toward the group. As she came into full view, Grissom suppressed a brief gasp at the yellow and purple discolorations around both of her cheekbones and the swelling of her lips. The smile she offered him was patronizing, and he couldn't figure out why. He didn't know it, but he was looking at a tougher Wendy Gardner than the one who had sat fecklessly in Cavalier Books the afternoon before—a Wendy Gardner who knew that you could be hit in the face without it being the end of the world, and that you could feel lousy about doing something and still have it be the right thing to do.

"You look like you got worked over pretty good," Grissom said.

"You oughta see the other guy," Wendy replied, upgrading the smile from patronizing to gamely joshing. She tossed a folded piece of white paper into Stevens's lap. "I'm supposed to give that to you."

Stevens picked the paper up and read it: " 'Warden, we seem to have lost transmission from camera number six at B-4.' That's the signal?" Stevens asked then, glancing up at Michaelson.

Michaelson nodded.

"Freeze all cameras at B-4," Stevens said.

"What is this?" Grissom demanded. "Community theater?"

"Reenactment," Michaelson told him. "We have the warden's kind cooperation. All right. We are now at the point we had reached on the afternoon of the killing, when Warden Stevens learned for the first time that something might be wrong. Why don't we run the Supply Room tape back and see what we have."

"We already know what the Supply Room tape for that afternoon shows," Grissom protested.

"I'm not talking about that tape," Michaelson said. "I'm talking about the tape that's been running for the last several minutes, while we've been talking."

Stevens nodded toward the guard sitting at the portable console and monitor. After a few key punches, the monitor screen filled with an image. Everyone in the area strained to look at it.

On the screen appeared a head, shoulders and chest shot of Desmond Gardner, face to face with the viewer. After two to three seconds, a toy dart flew into the picture. Its suction cup struck Gardner in the center of the forehead. He began to pitch forward. Snow abruptly replaced the image on the screen.

"Well," Michaelson said, "it would appear that there's something in the Supply Room that would bear investigation."

Stevens led the group a few steps to the door. Smith opened it. Looking into the room, the assemblage saw Desmond Gardner lying in the far corner of the room, diagonally across from the door and the corner where the surveillance camera was. He lay in front of the cream-colored tarpaulin draped over what they all knew to be the mirror taken from Smith's office. In the middle of the room lay a child's black plastic dart gun, a pair of work gloves and a second dart.

"The second dart represents the shell casing, of course," Michaelson said. "The analogy is a bit inexact, but it was the best we could do."

"Of course," Stevens said sarcastically.

"Hmm," Grissom said.

"Can we agree," Michaelson asked then, "that in its essentials this scene duplicates the one Officer Smith described and that, for that matter, the rest of us eventually saw that afternoon?"

"I don't see anything wrong with it," Smith said.

"Nor do I," Stevens agreed.

"Okay," Grissom shrugged.

"Very well. Can we also agree that there is no one else in

185

this room at the moment, and that no one has come out of it during the period that all of us have had it under surveillance?"

This question drew three affirmatives.

"Clearly, moreover, the dart could have been a bullet. If you accept my representation that this tape segment didn't begin running until some point well after our discussion down here began, it follows, doesn't it, that former Senator Gardner today—and therefore Mr. Martinelli earlier this week—could have been killed by someone who wasn't in the room with him?"

"It does," Grissom admitted. "But I don't see how. Unless there was a trap gun or something . . . ."

"In the case of this reenactment, fortunately, we have another tape taking a somewhat longer view of the event, in both senses of the term." Michaelson glanced up at the surveillance camera. The others followed his look, and saw that a twin camera was mounted next to it. "Let's go review that one, shall we? Oh, and inasmuch as we have exhausted the possibilities of former Senator Gardner's thespian contributions, perhaps he could be allowed to join us."

They walked back to the portable monitor, joined this time by Gardner. The guard attending the monitor punched some more buttons and presently the screen again filled with an image.

The screen once more showed Desmond Gardner's head, shoulders and chest, face on, against a neutral background. Once more a dart flew into the picture, and once more it struck him in the forehead. Again, he pitched forward. This time the image didn't stop.

They saw Gardner fall all the way to the floor, sprawled on his stomach. Then they saw the body moving toward the camera.

"What the hell?" Grissom muttered.

The body continued to move toward the camera, as if on a conveyor belt. Then, as it progressed, the neutral background suddenly dropped from the top of the screen to the bottom, revealing cinder blocks that looked dark gray on the black-and-white picture.

"This couldn't get any nuttier," Grissom said.

Which, however, it immediately did. A second image of the body appeared on the screen, on an apparent collision course with the first. The second body was lying with its head away from the camera. As it moved, it went farther from the camera while the first body continued to come closer to the camera.

"It's a mirror!" Grissom said. "But . . . ."

"Keep watching," Michaelson said.

It was now quite clear that they were watching an image recorded by a camera shooting into a mirror. The bodies lay head to head, the nearer one with its feet toward the camera and the farther with its feet away. Then the first body disappeared for a moment and the second body seemed to be lifted partly into the air. A whitish blur moved behind and beneath it. The body flopped and then settled back to the floor, now facing more or less toward the camera. It was now feet to feet with its mirror image.

"But four different people at least saw . . . ."

"Keep watching."

A plastic tube came into the picture. A fine spray came out of the tube for several seconds, directed at the mirror. When the spraying ended, an opaque blotch marred the upper third of the mirror.

The tube withdrew. There was another whitish blur and the mirror disappeared behind a tarpaulin draped over it. Now the camera saw only one simulated corpse, lying in front of a neutral background. The last important things the camera picked up were the dart gun, dart and gloves dropping onto the floor of the Supply Room.

"Theory," Michaelson said. "Martinelli came into the Supply Room in anticipation of meeting the Honor Cottage's supplier of contraband pharmaceuticals there. Naturally, he didn't stand in full view of the camera but, on the contrary, directly underneath the camera, where he expected to be out of the camera's range. He was surprised to see the mirror uncovered and unblotched but, before he could appreciate the implications of this situation he was even more surprised to see a pistol being pointed at him from the other side of the bars on the window—that is, from outside the Honor Cottage. The killer, who was at the window outside the room, instantly shot Martinelli. The killer then shot the camera lens, which prevented the camera from recording any more images but didn't prevent it from continuing to transmit the electronic noise it was recording to the video-taperecorder in the Administration Building."

"Why didn't anyone else in the prison hear this fusillade?" Billikin asked.

CO-2 Wesson Smith shook his head condescendingly at the desk jockey's ignorance.

"A .22 pistol makes a noise a bit louder than a cap gun, but anyone whose idea of a gunshot is the racket you get with a .38 or a .45 wouldn't associate the sounds this peashooter made with gunshots."

"Especially," Michaelson added, "if much of the noise had wide open spaces to escape into instead of four stone walls to bounce off of."

"Why did the Supply Room camera only pick up the image in the mirror, instead of picking up the frame and the area beside and behind the mirror as well?" Stevens asked.

"Because the killer adjusted the camera lens beforehand so that its field of vision was limited to the reflective surface of the mirror," Michaelson said.

"And why didn't the crack scene-of-crime team spot that rather unusual adjustment—something you'd hardly expect in a surveillance camera?"

"Because they were looking at a camera that had had a bullet shot through its lens. The bullet would represent an at least superficially plausible explanation for anything else about the lens that seemed unusual."

"All right," Grissom scowled. "Go on then."

"Very well," Michaelson said. "In preparation for the murder, the killer had taken the tarpaulin off the mirror and tucked one edge of it behind the camera mount bracket, stretching the rest of the tarpaulin down the wall and along the floor. He had attached monofilament fishing line—very nearly invisible to the naked eye, much less on videotape—to the grommets in the tarpaulin and to the transmission jack. Once Martinelli was dead and the camera lens shattered by gunfire, the killer pulled the tarpaulin along the floor. This pulled Martinelli's body along with it. When the killer had gotten Martinelli all the way across the floor, he pulled the tarpaulin up, dumping Martinelli's body off of it and reorienting it."

"You see?" Billikin said to Grissom. "You should've been looking for someone whose hands were cut to ribbons by pulling a 180-pound weight with monofilament fishing line."

"The gentleman was wearing gloves," Michaelson commented mildly.

"Anyway," Wendy said, "if he did it the way I did, he didn't pull it hand over hand. He wrapped the line around a plywood two by four and just turned the board over and over."

"The next part's the one I wanna hear," Grissom said.

"The next part is pretty much as you saw. The killer stuck a fertilizer spritzer tube through the window and sprayed potassium phosphate and calcium, a fairly common liquid fertilizer, on the mirror. This created the opaque blotch that we all saw. The killer then threw the tarp back over the mirror, threw the gun, shell casings and work gloves into the middle of the room, and went on about his business."

"Wait a minute," Smith said. "Your theory doesn't explain how the gun got into the Honor Cottage without activating the metal detector, any more than the other theory does. All openings to the outside are equipped with a metal detector tied to the alarm, including that window."

"An excellent point," Michaelson conceded. "The answer is that the killer waited until the alarm had already been activated by inmate Banich's attempt to enter through the front door with a bolt in his pocket—a bolt that I expect the killer *found* and gave to Ganich to bring back in, counting on Banich's carelessness about the metal detector to result in Banich's effort triggering the alarm. As soon as the killer heard that alarm ringing, he tossed the gun and shell casings into the room, and the consequent alarm was covered by the one Banich inadvertently activated. Metaphorically as well as literally, in other words, the killer did it with mirrors."

"That gets the gun and bullets inside B-4," Smith conceded. "How did they get inside the facility as a whole?"

"How does cocaine get in? How does contraband of any kind get in? No prison on earth is airtight. Besides, we know that, somehow or other, the gun and bullets got into the prison. They're here. The pertinent question is *when* they got inside Honor Cottage B-4. I think that the explanation I'm suggesting is the most plausible."

"Except for one thing," Grissom said. "At least four people saw the blotch on the mirror before the killing. The mirror had to be perfectly clean at the time of the killing in order for your theory to work. Otherwise, the blotch would have shown up on the image recorded by the camera."

"Exactly right. And the mirror was clean at the time of the killing, because between the time Officer Smith and the others saw the blotch and the time of the murder, the killer cleaned the blotch off."

"Hold it," Smith interjected. "I tried to rub that blotch off myself the first time I saw it and couldn't do it. And Stepanski told me that stain on the mirror was between the glass and the silver and could only be cleaned by disassembling the mirror to clean behind the glass."

"He did indeed tell you that," Michaelson said. "But the fact is that while potassium phosphate and calcium in solution can't just be rubbed off once it has dried, it can be cleaned off with ammonia and muscle. Much as I hate to cast aspersions on someone who's not here to defend himself, I'm very much afraid that, in addition to murdering Sweet Tony Martinelli, inmate Stepanski deliberately misled you when he made the statement you allude to."

"Stepanski?" the FBI agent and Smith said at once.

"I don't really see any way around it," Michaelson said. "He was the one with the access to the Supply Room required to make all of the elaborate preparations—the mirror, the tarpaulin, the fishing line and so forth. He's the one we know was outside at the time of the killing. I'm very much afraid that he's the one who murdered Martinelli."

"But why?" Grissom demanded. "We have a motive for Gardner, a motive for Squires, maybe even a motive for Lanier if we assume he and Martinelli had some kind of dispute on a drug deal. Stepanski was buddies with everybody. What conceivable motive did he have?"

"Let's take that question one step at a time," Michaelson said. "First, why was Martinelli, a violent, vicious criminal, assigned to an honor cottage in a minimum security facility?"

"No comment," Stevens said. Billikin and Grissom murmured assents.

"My theory on that is that Martinelli had made a deal. His role in arranging a fraudulent sugar import scam had come to light in the course of an investigation stimulated by sources we won't go into."

"I thought you said Martinelli was a violent criminal," Grissom objected.

"He was. A violent criminal from Miami. As such, he was in touch with the Miami criminal underground, many of whose members are Cuban. So is the Castro government, many of whose members are also Cuban. When the Cuban government had occasion to do business with a New Orleans gangster named Gunderson, the natural way to do so was therefore through his principal Miami employee, who I suspect was Martinelli."

"Why do you suspect that?" Stevens asked.

"Because the photograph found in Martinelli's room suggests that he had information tying him to Gunderson. But we digress. That Martinelli was exposed in the course of this investigation is a matter of public record. I have hypothesized a deal: that he would do short and easy time at a place like this, and in exchange would give the United States the evidence necessary to nail Gunderson. This bargain was particularly appealing from the government's viewpoint, because housing Martinelli in these quarters seemed a cheap way to keep him safe."

"Well," Grissom said. "That part certainly worked out, didn't it?"

"The best laid plans, etc. These particular plans went seriously off the rails, I suspect, because someone in the New Orleans syndicate had made a substantial and as yet not repaid loan to a construction company still owned by Stepanski and his brother. I don't know for sure what happened. My guess is this: Gunderson, suspecting what was afoot, bought the paper from whichever of his colleagues held it; he then let Stepanski know that if Stepanski got rid of Martinelli, all would be forgiven as far as the loan was concerned. Events suggest that that was enough for Stepanski."

"Even if it weren't enough, Stepanski had another motive," Desmond Gardner said quietly.

"What's that?" Stevens asked.

"Stepanski's other brother died of AIDS. That was the start of the spiral that ended up landing Stepanski in here and getting his company in hock to the mob in the first place. Martinelli was a queenmaker, as the allusion to Squires's motive a while back indicated."

"What are you talking about?" Smith asked.

"I caught Martinelli shortly before he was killed essentially threatening to rape Squires," Gardner explained. "Stepanski knew about everything that went on in here. I believe he would've killed Martinelli for the sheer pleasure of watching him die."

"That much accepted," Michaelson said, "the rest follows

fairly easily. The gun and bullets were never inside the Honor Cottage. They were smuggled to a spot outside where Stepanski could retrieve them and use them. He did. I don't know if you can prove it, but I'm confident that that's the way it happened."

"But Stepanski was taking one hell of a chance," Grissom said. "At any moment while he was setting things up someone could have flipped on the monitor for that camera and caught him. For that matter, if that monitor had been flipped on during your guided tour ten minutes before it was, the alarm would have sounded ten minutes earlier and Stepanski would've been caught red-handed in the middle of his cover up."

"He certainly was taking a chance," Michaelson agreed. "But he had a lot to gain. Even if he's caught, as long as he doesn't betray Gunderson, his brother will be off the hook, with a life to lead and a business to run."

"Besides," said Billikin, who found the discussion had veered in a direction he knew something about, "what real choice did he have? If he didn't find some way to take care of the mob loan, the most he could possibly hope for once he got out of prison would be a chance for him and his kid brother to work the debt off as crack mules until they were both either dead or locked up for forty years."

"If you ask Stepanski," Desmond Gardner said, "I expect he'll tell you it was a good trade."

"I'll tell you what other choice he had," Grissom barked. "Go ahead and whack Martinelli exactly the way he did it, except shoot the camera first and skip the mirror and the tarp and all the other French pastry. What'd he gain from this elaborate charade you're talking about?"

"An alibi," Michaelson said. "He turned the strengths of the security system against that very system. He set the murder up to look as if it had to have been committed by someone inside the cottage, when Stepanski was indisputably outside the cottage. Whoever was blamed for the killing, Stepanski quite reasonably hoped that he'd be cleared."

"You're saying that to give himself a hope of being cleared of murder, he did a whole series of things that incredibly increased the chance that he'd be spotted doing something that would get him convicted of murder," Grissom said skeptically.

"He increased that chance marginally, not incredibly," Michaelson said. "Once he had adjusted the Supply Room camera lens to a tight focus on the mirror, the actually incriminating conduct that that camera could record would be limited to a relatively short time period. There are 112 cameras around this facility, most with a higher viewing priority than the six here in Honor Cottage B-4. There are six monitors in the Administration Building. The odds against Stepanski being spotted on one of those monitors were therefore greater than eighteen to one—not bad, when what's at stake is the chance to lead a decent life once he gets out."

"But the odds against him being spotted on the monitor in Officer Smith's quarters here in the Honor Cottage were only six to one," Billiken said.

"I'm afraid they were somewhat longer," Michaelson said. "You see, Officer Smith is a very conscientious and systematic operative. Stepanski knew for certain that at the time he had in mind for the murder Officer Smith would be making his rounds, and not monitoring the six B-4 cameras."

"All right, all right," Grissom said. "Let's say I buy all that. What's the link between Martinelli's killing and this Cox character who apparently did such a number on the young lady here last night?"

"You'll recall that that was my second point," Michaelson said. "Having established that former Senator Gardner wasn't the killer, I hope I've persuaded you to devote the resources allocated to this case to finding out precisely what that link is. All I can do is guess."

"Try a guess on me," Grissom said.

Michaelson glanced at his watch. It was 1:32 and, in any event, Grissom's comment made it clear that Cox had already begun making interesting noises to the government.

"Fair enough," Michaelson said. "Cox kept track of questionable activities by members of Congress, including former Senator Gardner. Let's assume charitably that at first he did this merely as a form of employment insurance. Gunderson had compromised Senator Gardner. Therefore, Cox knew about Gunderson and perhaps even had tried to peddle to Gunderson information about other members of Congress."

"It sounds like a good guess so far. Keep going."

"Okay. Now, let's say you're Gunderson and you need someone to manipulate a sugar quota so that you can take advantage of an intriguing entrepreneurial opportunity. There aren't any members of Congress for sale to you, especially after Senator Gardner's unfortunate experience, so your best choice is to suborn a staffer of either one of the relevant committees or one of the members of those committees. Fortunately, based on your recent experience, you know at least one appropriately placed staffer who's eminently subornable."

"Cox," Grissom said.

"Exactly. In case you need something extra to make him see things your way, you inquire about him among your colleagues in organized crime in the Washington area and learn that he has a sexual taste that he wouldn't care to have revealed to all of the insiders in this gossip-happy, scandal-loving city—something risible involving spurs, leather boots, gauntlets and that type of thing. You make him aware of this knowledge and you have him where you want him."

"You certainly have," Billikin agreed.

"Martinelli of course knows about this as well as Gunderson. A photograph that he retained suggesting possession of that knowledge was found in his room after his murder," Michaelson said.

"Why did he hang onto that?"

"I'm speculating," Michaelson said, "but I'd say he hung onto it in case he needed to make another deal. I suspect he would've thought that it's the kind of thing he'd rather have than not have."

"That seems plausible," Billikin commented. "So you're saying that Gunderson used Cox to manipulate the sugar quota allocations so that Cuba could very slightly reduce the cost to the Soviets of propping up the Cuban economy by selling sugar to the United States."

"I was asked to guess," Michaelson remarked, "and that's my guess. The object being, of course, not to save a relatively small amount of money for the Soviet Union but to gain a relatively large amount of money for the underworld entrepreneurs involved. Those involved weren't selling out their country, they were duping that country's bureaucracy. The bureaucrats regard the latter as an infinitely greater sin—almost as grave as publicly revealing the fact that they have been duped."

CHAPTER 23

"There's media here," the intense young man whispered ungrammatically but accurately to the equally intense, slightly older woman standing in between him and Michaelson.

"What'd you expect?" the woman responded, talking as if she hoped to make the words come out without actually moving her lips.

The young man was from the lowest level of the White House staff above speech writers. The young woman was from the Public Affairs Office of the United States Department of Justice.

"There's not going to be any trouble with this is there?" the young man asked Michaelson.

"He knows what the deal is, right?" the young woman asked.

"There isn't any *deal*," the young man hissed.

"Former Senator Gardner understands the situation," Michaelson said placidly. "I understand the situation. Wendy Gardner understands the situation. We have each given our word and we will each keep our word. No leaks to the press about the sugar business, no attempt to revive former Senator Gardner's elective career, and if anyone asks us neither promise made on the strength of any assurance of action by the executive branch."

"I'm still shaky about that last part," the young man said to the young woman. "About him not running for public office,

I mean. I'm not even sure that's constitutional. I can just see him going into court a couple of years from now and rubbing some judge's nose in the First Amendment."

"I reviewed the research myself," the young woman said. "The power specified in Article II, section 2, paragraph 1 of the Constitution is derived directly from the analogous power of English kings. The legal maxim governing their power was *non sub homine sed sub Deo et lege: Let the King be under no man but under God and the Law.*' "

"That sort of begs the question then, doesn't it?" the young man asked.

"Take my word for it. We're okay."

"I still . . . ."

"Quiet. Here they come."

Senator Desmond Gardner, wearing a navy blue suit and tie, smiling and looking fit, stepped through the door of the Guard House at Fritchieburg onto the parking lot. Wendy Gardner walked just behind him and to his left, beside her mother. Warden Stevens trailed them slightly. After they were all well into the parking lot, Stevens circled around to come abreast of Gardner. Everyone took this as a signal to stop. Stevens held out his hand.

"Good luck," he said. "I hope I never see you again, at least in a professional capacity."

"Thank you," Gardner said as he shook the warden's hand. "You won't."

Stevens turned on his heel and strode back toward the Guard House. The Gardners started forward again, walking toward a white stretch limousine that Marjorie Randolph had hired for the occasion. Two casually dressed people with tape-recorders—what the intense young man had referred to as the media—hurried up to the trio.

"Senator Gardner, how does it feel to be leaving prison?"

"Very good."

"Is it true that the pardon is conditioned on your never seeking elective office again?"

"I will not under any circumstances run for any office at any level. That's my personal choice and irrevocable decision. How that fits in with what the legal papers say is a question I'm not qualified to answer." All spoken with a knowing smile and a philosophical expression. He was still a consummate master of the art.

"What will you be doing now?"

"Trying to make it up to my family and community for letting them down the way I did."

"The pardon message talked about 'extraordinary services to the cause of law and justice.' What's that a reference to?"

"That's between me and the President. If you folks'll excuse me, I know you've got deadlines and this big car here's costing someone a lot of money every minute we stand around talking."

Gardner ducked into the car behind his wife and daughter. The chauffeur closed the door behind them. Marjorie had been waiting in the car, and Michaelson had taken advantage of the impromptu press conference to slip inobtrusively in the other side.

"Baloney sandwiches and beer tonight?" Michaelson asked Marjorie.

"Not tonight. Tonight calls for something a bit more celebratory. Pizza and red wine, I think."

"Marjorie, you have yourself a date."

The limousine maneuvered smoothly through the gate, negotiated the speed bumps and found the open highway. Gardner, beaming, settled back in the thickly cushioned seat.

"Richard, thank you for everything."

"My pleasure."

He clapped his hands together.

"Now, young lady," he said to Wendy, "we need to have a talk."

"About what?"

"About census tracts."

"What about them?"

"They show that average household income was barely

stable and trending downward in Henry Simmons's district, which happens to be where you officially live."

"Who's Henry Simmons?"

"He's your state legislator. More important, he's a politician whose base is changing and who isn't paying any attention to it. He's the political equivalent of a Potemkin Village. Election after next he'll be eminently beatable, as long as someone who knows what they're doing runs against him."

"But dad, you promised that you . . . ."

"Who said anything about me? I'm talking about you."

"Dad, don't be ridiculous. I'm nineteen years old."

"The perfect age to become recording secretary of the 23rd District Party Club."

"I'm not even a member."

"Yes you are. I paid your dues myself."

"But I don't know anyone in that club."

"I know plenty of people in it."

"Dad . . . ."

"Don't get me wrong. You'll have to work hard. You'll have to pay your dues, and I don't mean with money. But it'll be worth it. Simmons is getting a pass next year, and four years after that he'll be ripe for the plucking. You'll be twenty-four and your last name'll be Gardner. It'll be perfect. He's vulnerable on abortion and gun control."

"I'm not going to cut and trim on abortion, dad. I feel too strongly about it."

"That's okay," Gardner chuckled. "Gun control should be plenty, all by itself."

Wendy turned away from her father and looked out the window. She smiled and then started to giggle. She lowered her head, held it in her hands, and shook for a moment with silent, helpless laughter. Then she raised her head and looked back at her father.

"You don't have any strong moral objection to making the appropriate noises about gun control, do you?" Gardner asked.

"Well," Wendy said, shrugging and smiling thoughtfully, "everything's relative, isn't it?"

———